"Don't I Have Any Say In This?"

Trish demanded. "What if I want to go home *right now?*"

"Well . . ." Zach paused. "If we had a telephone, and if you were feeling *very* brave, you could call a Tijuana taxi, but . . ." He shrugged, letting the words trail off.

He was right, she realized. She had brought nothing with her. No bags, no purse, no money. She had the clothes on her back—a slinky, strapless evening gown—and nothing more. She was in a foreign country without money, accompanied by a man of suspicious character with whom she felt burgeoning fears, wild desires and precious little control. She was a sitting duck!

Dear Reader:

SILHOUETTE DESIRE is an exciting new line of contemporary romances from Silhouette Books. During the past year, many Silhouette readers have written in telling us what other types of stories they'd like to read from Silhouette, and we've kept these comments and suggestions in mind in developing SILHOUETTE DESIRE.

DESIREs feature all of the elements you like to see in a romance, plus a more sensual, provocative story. So if you want to experience all the excitement, passion and joy of falling in love, then SILHOUETTE DESIRE is for you.

Karen Solem
Editor-in-Chief
Silhouette Books

SUZANNE FORSTER
Undercover Angel

Silhouette Desire

Published by Silhouette Books New York

America's Publisher of Contemporary Romance

SILHOUETTE BOOKS
300 E. 42nd St., New York, N.Y. 10017

Copyright © 1985 by Suzanne Forster

Distributed by Pocket Books

ISBN: 0-373-05215-4

First Silhouette Books printing June, 1985

10 9 8 7 6 5 4 3 2 1

America's Publisher of Contemporary Romance

Printed in the U.S.A.

SUZANNE FORSTER

started her writing career by accident. Literally. She took up writing while confined to bed after a car accident, and her first published book was discovered quite accidentally by an editor who read it while judging the finalists in the 1984 Romance Writers of America writing contest. Accidents do happen, but Ms. Forster's talent is the real key to her success.

1

The swish of glass revolving doors propelled Patricia McCallister out onto the Great Western Bank Building's rain-soaked marble entrance. At ten after five, Wilshire Boulevard pulsed, alive with rush-hour traffic.

"Wait!" she called. Clutching her garment bag and leather tote, she waved a closed umbrella and ran after a departing Yellow cab. "Wait!" Her breath came in short gasps as she stopped at the corner and watched the taxi speed away. Swearing quietly, she raised her umbrella against the persistent drizzle.

Several more cabs accelerated through the intersection despite her waves and two-fingered whistles. Urgency tingled in Trish's stomach. As she paced the curb nervously, an ominous rumbling came from behind her. Startled, she turned and jumped back, but not fast enough. An RTD bus thundered past, spraying great waves of grimy water and drenching her in the process.

Dripping and infuriated, she shook herself like an

insulted cat. She'd get a taxi, by damn, if she had to shoot out its tires with her deadly black handgun. Despite her fury, the idea tickled her. It was hardly deadly, but the rubber dime-store weapon she'd bought after taking a women's self-defense class had discouraged a would-be mugger once.

As she hastily brushed at her sodden clothing, a dented green cab, its top light off, skidded into the intersection and stopped just as the signal went red. "Thank God," Trish murmured. Hurrying toward it, she stepped into the street, carefully avoiding the murky runoff that rushed along the gutter. Shifting the umbrella to her left hand, she reached for the old Plymouth's back-door handle. It jiggled like a loose tooth and nearly came off in her hand. Twisting it gingerly, she opened the door and gasped as a tumble of empty cardboard boxes landed at her feet.

"Hey! What're you doing, lady?" a surly voice yelled. "Shut that door!"

Baffled, Trish peered into the backseat's cardboard jungle. No room for a passenger in there, she decided hastily. Craning her neck, she tried to catch a glimpse of the completely obscured cabbie. "Okay if I sit up front?" she inquired hopefully. "I only need to go as far as—"

"NO!" the voice boomed. "I'm off duty! *Shut that door!*"

Startled, Trish forced the unruly cardboard containers back into the cab, gave the door a quick swing and watched it mercilessly crush an escaping box.

An instant later, determination bested fear. She *had* to get to the Brentmoor. If she put it off even one more day, her courage might fail her. She tried the front-door handle. It held fast. Through the rain-blurred window, she saw the cabbie shake his head and motion her away.

"Hey! Come on—*please*," she blurted as the light turned green and the blocked traffic began to honk. "It's important! Please! I have to—"

The taxi started to pull away.

"Stop!" Trish screamed. "Stop!" Clutching the door handle, she ran along beside the cab.

"Jeez—lady!" came the cabbie's muffled roar as he abruptly braked. The old Plymouth lurched toward the curb and shuddered to a stop.

Horns blared, and a frustrated driver thrust his head out a car window and screamed an obscenely imaginative threat.

The window Trish squinted through began to creak open. The driver's angry silver eyes, flaring nostrils and clenched teeth greeted her. "Lady, you may have a death wish, but I don't," he snarled. "Now get the hell away from my cab, and let me get out of here before that mob kills us both."

Trish knew the dangers of provoking crazed L.A. rush-hour commuters, but she'd have to take the risk. Holding on so tight her fingers burned, she firmly shook her head.

A barrage of oaths carried over revving engines. A car door slammed with a loud crack. The cabdriver looked back, then quickly unlocked the front door and pushed it open. "Get in," he ordered. "Now!"

Struggling to close the umbrella, Trish slid in and pulled her bags behind her. Before she had the door shut, they were accelerating down Wilshire Boulevard.

She started to thank him, but noting the vigorous scowl on his face, thought better of it. No matter, she resolved blithely, checking her watch. Five twenty-eight. Her plan was now operational. Once she'd changed her clothes and arrived at the Brentmoor, all she had to do was get past security and Anton Gregory was fair game! Renowned artist, aesthete, and owner of a string of galleries, he was the man she had chosen to launch her earthbound art career. *Anton Gregory would elude her no longer.*

She reached down for her garment bag and froze, suddenly aware of a serious glitch in her strategy. Knowing she'd be pressed for time, she'd planned to change surreptitiously in the cab's backseat. What would she do now? Use the front seat? With him next to her? *Oh Lord.* She could ask him to stop while she changed at a gas station. But was there time? And would he wait?

A harsh voice cut into her preoccupation. "The next time I stop for a light, you get out—understand?" the cabbie ordered with a burning glance.

"But—" About to protest, she realized the flinty set of his features required a more subtle strategy. Best not to mention the gas station until the last moment, she decided shrewdly. "Oh, please," she entreated, all helpless femininity. "I only need to go as far as the Brentmoor. It's just a few blocks off Wilshire."

"The Brentmoor Country Club?" An eyebrow shot up as he glanced at her with some interest. "Now, that's a coincidence. I'm headed there myself."

"Really?" Relief washed over her. "But hardly a coincidence. Kismet," she said, laughing. "Somebody up there knew our destination and brought us together."

His features visibly relaxed. "The great carpooler in the sky?"

She smiled, a spark of hope warming her. If everything went according to plan, she might even be able to resign her administrative assistant position at Grover Chemicals. Oh, how she'd love to serve up her resignation along with her stuffy boss's morning coffee!

As the traffic thickened and slowed, her smile faded. I don't have time for a traffic jam, she worried, checking her watch again. If I don't arrive within the hour, he'll be gone.

"You in a hurry?" the cabbie queried casually. "Meeting someone there?"

"Yes—I mean—*no.* I mean yes, I'm in a hurry, and no—I'm not meeting someone there . . . exactly." An impulse to confide in him was interrupted as static broke from the dashboard speaker. Noticing that the cab's meter wasn't running, she watched him snatch up the microphone.

While carrying on a fuzzy, crackling conversation with a female voice, he guided the old taxi into a faster lane, expertly negotiating through the snarled traffic with one hand. Incredible, she thought, experiencing a flash of awe as he calmly traversed lanes, weaving through cars, vans and semis and taking advantage of every opening. He's good at this.

Watching him, she realized he was startlingly attractive . . . but years too young. Probably twenty-three or twenty-four, she decided almost wistfully. It seemed ironic that at thirty-four, she would see a man his age as so very young, so out of reach. Not that she had any intention of reaching.

His hair, a splash of golden sun-brushed blond, formed a halo of tousled curls all over his head. And although his face was only partially angled toward her, she observed an odd energy emanating from his silvery blue-flecked eyes as he mastered the road. Her artist's eye sought critical detachment as she secretly evaluated the linear planes of his jaw and subtly cleft chin. If Michael the Archangel had an earthly form, he could be sitting right next to me, she thought almost reverently. A painter's dream!

Returning the microphone to its hook, he brought the cab to a stop at a red light. As his eyes brushed over her, she felt a tug in her stomach. The vibrations coming her way were anything but angelic. This was a virile young man in his prime, she realized, feeling an involuntary shiver. Thank heavens she was no longer susceptible.

As she checked her watch again, her heart lost a beat. Stopping to change was definitely out of the question, but she'd never make it past the doorman without her camouflage. Her brain nearly jammed as she considered and discarded options.

She saw the signal flash green. The cab began to move. Lordy, she realized finally, her heart accelerating to double time, there's only one thing I can do.

"Excuse me," she said tentatively. He glanced around and she nearly jumped. Those uncanny eyes! Despite the tanned and golden innocence of youth, he looked positively treacherous. What if he was a pervert? She'd heard of rapes in taxicabs, hadn't she? They might even say she'd enticed him. She had her gun, but would it fool anyone at such close range? Tell him, Trisha, she commanded. "I have to change my clothes," she croaked nervously.

One eyebrow raised quizzically as if he wasn't at all sure what she meant. "There's a ladies' lounge at the Brentmoor," he offered finally.

She quelled her uncertainty with a brave, matter-of-fact smile. "I have to change *before* I get there." Unzipping the garment bag, she took out the jade green silk dress and laid it over the seat between them.

The cab lurched to a stop at another red light. Astonishment gripped his features. "You're going to change *here?*"

"Yes." She nodded quickly.

"In my front seat?"

"I'd prefer the back, but since it's full of boxes. . ." She resisted the impulse to ask him what kind of taxi driver loaded up his backseat with boxes. Why push her luck?

"Could you look away or something?" she requested politely, as he stared at her, mouth open, sun-bleached eyebrows meeting in an astonished vee.

"People don't change their clothes in taxicabs." He pointed at the green dress as if it were evidence, but his protest held little conviction. "What do you think this is? A mobile dressing room?"

"Please," she entreated. "Please, I have to. It's important. *Really.* My future hangs in the balance!"

Frowning, he dazedly turned away.

The light turned green, and as his attention was drawn back to the hazards of driving, she breathed a grateful sigh. About to lower her skirt, she peeked his way. He stared straight ahead, hands stiff on the steering wheel, looking as perplexed as a skeptic who'd just witnessed a miracle.

Good, she thought. He's off balance. Now if he'll only stay that way until I finish.

She removed her skirt and quickly covered herself with it. Piece of cake, she thought, feeling inexplicably naked even though she was still wearing her blouse and a lace-trimmed bra-slip underneath. But now for the real challenge. How did she get her blouse off without giving him and the rush-hour drivers a course in female anatomy? For the first time in her life she wished she were less amply endowed. In a situation like this, her generous breasts were just that much more area to cover.

Aware that the cab had slowed significantly, she pulled a compact out of her leather tote and quickly brushed the dark swirls of sable brown hair back from her face. Angling the mirror until she picked up his reflection, she saw his eyes moving restively.

His gaze veered from the front windshield to the seat between them and back again. Uh-oh, she thought, her stomach doing an odd cartwheel, he's coming out of it. The idea of a woman undressing right next to him is beginning to arouse his baser instincts. Hurry up, Trish, his mind is not on the road. He could be trouble!

In an attempt to create some cover, she took her skirt by its band, clamped it firmly between her teeth and let it cascade in front of her. Feeling rather clever, she began to unbutton the back of her blouse. Her fingers trembled violently. Damn buttonholes. Too small. Hurry!

Unfastening all but the last button, which refused to come free, she gave up and wiggled her arms out of the sleeves.

The taxi's sudden swerve into an adjoining lane sent her swaying like a willow in a windstorm. Cramped fingers worked frantically. There was no way to get the blouse over her head with that last button fastened! This is going to take at least two hands and maybe a crowbar, she realized, groaning. Her jaws ached and the jersey skirt tasted like wet, wadded tissues in her mouth. Giving up all hope of covering her lower extremities, she bent forward, arched like a gymnast and tackled the problem with both hands.

As the car jerked to a stop at an intersection, Trish pitched forward.

"Oh God, I'm sorry," the cabbie apologized hoarsely. He reached as though to help her restore her balance.

Straightening, she shook her head fiercely, feeling incredibly foolish as the skirt waggled back and forth. Growling, gurgling noises came from her throat. How could she make him see she didn't want *help*—she wanted him to turn the other way so she could finish!

Watching her, his face contorted with confused fascination. A deep flush colored his cheeks. His mouth parted, quivering somewhere between amazement and amusement, and his eyes narrowed as though he was trying to interpret her garbled noises. Then suddenly his uncertainty seemed to vanish. The lights in his quicksilver eyes were brilliant lasers. He cocked his head. "How about some help? Looks like you need a couple more hands—"

She unclenched her jaws to tell him to take a walk, and the skirt dropped to her lap. In that fateful instant, the button gave up its battle, and the blouse joined her skirt. Letting out a gasp, she grabbed for the skirt and clutched it to her breasts for cover.

Shock paralyzed them both for an instant. Their eyes fixed jointly on the creamy soft cleavage the skirt didn't quite cover, then met and held. In a reflexive movement, she crossed her arms, clamping the skirt to her body like a shield.

Red-hot slashes colored his face. He turned away and grasped the wheel.

"I don't need any help!" she blurted, weak and febrile.

"I do." His voice was husky and was rushing for

breath. "Get your clothes on before I go into cardiac arrest and die or something even worse."

Trish, feeling mortification crawl her body like a platoon of tiny-footed insects, hunched down in the seat and reached for the jade green dress. Still holding her cover in place, she pulled it over her head with one hand, then slipped the skirt out from underneath.

The cabbie sat staring rigidly out the side window, arms folded in a self-imposed straitjacket. Outside, horns brayed repeatedly. For one traumatic moment Trish thought it was because of her. Then, feeling giddy with relief, she realized the light had turned green. The honking was an impatient signal from the cars behind them.

As her taxi driver pulled forward, she zipped the jade silk up the back. *Dressed!* she thought exultantly. She felt better instantly. Covered, invulnerable, dry.

Rolling the damp clothes up in the plastic garment bag, she stuffed the bundle into her already over-crowded tote bag and struggled unsuccessfully to zip it shut.

They drove the next few blocks in thick silence. She tried valiantly to concentrate on the mission ahead of her, but the accidental intimacy with a man just two feet from her totally absorbed her thoughts. Curiosity about him itched like a maddening insect bite. Finally she could no longer resist a sly peripheral analysis of the patterns of golden hair and raised tendons that ran the length of his forearm as he gripped the steering wheel with sure hands. Probably pumps iron, she thought, feeling schoolgirl butterflies. Fascinated, she stole a sidelong glance at his body. No, not a weight lifter, she quickly decided. There was no extra bulk on that splendidly muscled frame. He looks bionic, she decided, marveling at the rippling energy that seemed to fill the space between them.

He made a right turn off Wilshire, then looked over at her, and although she still sensed waves of tension between them, he seemed, at least superficially, to have recovered. "You belong to the Brentmoor?" he asked conversationally.

"No . . . I've never been there before."

"You're a guest, then?"

She shook her head, then wondered if she should have fibbed. But why? She'd never see him again anyway.

The puzzled frustration that had marked his features ever since she first entered his cab reappeared. "How are you planning to get in?"

"I'll get in," she replied confidently.

"You sound pretty sure of yourself for someone who's never been in the place."

She contemplated her scheme with a swell of pleasure, then couldn't resist a self-satisfied disclosure. "I have a plan."

"A plan?" He glanced at her as one might a fantasizing child.

"That's right," she clipped out defensively. "It's foolproof."

"Foolproof?" He snorted. "Obviously you haven't met Jenkins, the doorman. Don't let the top hat and tails fool you. He's an urban guerrilla."

She regarded him with patient disdain. "I don't plan to fight my way in. Fortunately, even an urban guerrilla will respond to the right stimuli. Macho types, in particular"—she smiled at him with the superior wisdom of her years—"are so very predictable."

He stopped for a red light and turned to study her face. "Is this guy you want to see really worth all the trouble?"

"Why are you so sure it's a guy?"

"It's a guy all right and I'll bet he's rich. Either that or you're a high priced call gir—"

"High-priced *what*?"

"My." He winked as though he'd hit the target. "Aren't *we* touchy?"

Her dark eyes issued storm warnings. "I'm *not* a call girl," she insisted. "But I do happen to be

16

meeting an important man. Anton Gregory." she announced loftily.

"*Who?*" he exclaimed. "Why *him?*"

Realizing she'd already shown and told too much, she countered lightly, "Why not? He's good-looking, successful, very rich—"

"And married," he cut in.

"Separated," she corrected.

"Sounds pretty cold-blooded," he said accusingly. "I thought going after a guy for his bankroll went out with women's lib."

"Did it?" she replied evenly, baiting him. "Well, in that case, it's a lost art and I'm about to revive it. Mr. Gregory has cocktails at the Brentmoor several times a week. I happen to know he'll be there today."

"So why crash the Brentmoor? Why not just call his office and make an appointment?"

"I've been trying for months," she sighed, serious now, "and getting nowhere. This is a last-ditch effort." She looked out the side window and saw they were almost there. Her spine stiffened. Lord, she'd all but forgotten the rest of her plan. "Don't take me to the club's entrance yet," she said quietly. "There's something I have to do first."

"Okay." He shrugged. His expression was openly curious as he stopped at the guard gate and waved to the uniformed security man. "Hi, Tom," he called. "My fare's a guest at the club."

Trish held her breath. How could she have forgotten about the guard gate?

Tom obviously knew her taxi driver. He smiled and waved them through.

Close, Trish, she scolded herself, very close.

They continued along the semicircular drive until the ivy-covered Georgian mansion that served as a clubhouse came into view, then pulled over and stopped fifty feet from the entry's red canvas arcade.

Trish swiftly found the pink balloon in her tote bag and blew it up to a soft, squishy, underinflated six-inch round. As she started to pull up her loose-fitting silk dress, his hand caught her wrist. "I don't believe it. Are you taking your clothes off again?"

"Do you mind?" she inquired primly. Pushing his hand away, she lifted the dress and pinned the balloon by its knotted end to her slip, positioning it over her stomach. She pulled the dress down and inspected herself as much as she could in the cramped quarters. Satisfied, she took out her compact, went about some badly needed repairs, then retrieved a two and one-half carat simulated-diamond wedding set and a gem-studded cocktail ring from a small brocade case in her purse. She completed the sparkling ensemble with a diamond-encrusted Lucien Picard wristwatch, the only authentic piece she owned. Suppressing a grimace, she viewed her bejeweled hands. Not at all her style, but she wanted no doubts as to her financial status.

"There," she said, replacing the compact and smoothing out her dress. "How do I look?"

He quickly assessed her new contours, then shook his head dazedly. "Who's the father? The Goodyear blimp?"

"Drop me off at the entrance," she ordered brusquely, to discourage more repartee. She had no doubt he'd try to dissuade her if given the chance. But she had her reasons for what she was doing, and she didn't need his approval. Not his, not anyone's. Trish McCallister was using her head for once. This was her shot at happiness. She only regretted all the sadly misspent years and the time it had taken to piece together her fragile self-esteem.

"Good luck," he whispered, surprising her, as he leaned over to open her door before the doorman reached them.

Mindful of her added girth, she carefully exited the cab and started up the red-carpeted walkway. Passing the imperious doorman, she nodded politely. "How do you do, Jenkins?"

"Excuse me, ma'am." He raised a hesitant white-gloved hand.

"What is it?" She smiled, tilting her chin and affecting studied elegance.

As he approached, she took a shaky sideways step and raised her hand to her forehead. "Oh—something's wrong," she said breathlessly. "I feel rather strange." She managed another hesitant step toward him, then wobbled precariously.

"Ma'am?" He took hold of her arm as she swayed.

"I'll be all right," she insisted weakly. But as she tried to stand on her own, a tremulous sigh escaped her throat, and she crumpled to the ground.

Stretched out gracefully on the carpeting, Trish listened to the commotion around her. The doorman checked for a pulse at her wrist and then rushed in to get the club's majordomo, who gave orders to have her taken to the ladies' lounge while he paged a doctor. "I'll carry her," offered a third male voice that she immediately recognized as her taxi driver's. Damn—was he still there? It was all she could do not to sit up and tell him to go away. Why had she ever confided in him? He could so easily sabotage her plan.

She felt herself being lifted by a pair of strong, sure arms and pressed close to a warm body, so close that her balloon drifted over to the side. Hoping no one would notice, she wriggled slightly, thinking to coax her tummy back to its original position. "Hey—" her carrier whispered. "Hold still."

"I'll see the ladies' lounge is cleared," announced the majordomo, his voice haughty and fretful. "Follow me—we'll take the back hallway. We don't want to horrify our guests."

The bumping and jostling of being carried continued until Trish felt herself lowered to a couch. She opened one eye just enough to see walls of mirrors and white satin brocade furniture. The ladies' lounge. Two pairs of male legs flanked the couch.

"Do you think she's going to give birth?" The majordomo's tone implied he'd rather witness World War III.

"No," her taxi driver reassured lightly. "I don't think there's any danger of that."

"Well—" He sighed petulantly. "I suppose someone should be here until the doctor comes. Would you mind staying a bit longer?"

"My pleasure."

Trish peeked and saw the majordomo hesitate at the door, then turn back. "You wouldn't happen to know her name, would you? Apparently she's someone's guest. I really must notify them."

"Sorry," came the congenial reply.

Trish's eyes popped open as the door closed. A handsome face smiled down at her. "Congratulations." His mild laughter was deferential. "You're in. Now what?"

He veered away as she sprang up, reached under her dress, and unpinned the balloon. After deflating and discarding it, she whirled around. "Now—you're leaving. Hurry, there's not much time!"

"Can't. You heard the main man. I'm under orders to stay until—"

"Leave!" She pointed emphatically toward the door.

Poised like a drill sergeant, she saw the door open. A tall, spare, white-haired man stepped in and froze at the sight of Trish's extended digit.

"I'm Dr. Birmingham," he explained, looking from Trish to the cabbie warily. "I was told there was a woman in need of medical aid in the ladies' lounge."

"Yes." She nodded quickly, lowering her arm in one self-conscious swoop. "She is—I mean, I am—or rather, I was . . . feeling quite faint. I'm fine now, though. Perfectly fine."

"I see." The doctor's eyes examined her from across the room. "I was also told that this woman was—"

He gaped at her stomach. Feeling an instant's panic, Trish, too, dropped her eyes, then met his and straightened indignantly. "I *beg* your pardon?" she challenged, a genteel eyebrow lifting imperiously.

The doctor shifted awkwardly. "Apparently I was given the wrong information." His thin smile encompassed both Trish and her companion. "Is there anything I can do . . . for either of you?"

"No, Doctor." She smiled graciously. "Thank you. Now if *both* you gentlemen would be kind enough to leave? I'd like to freshen up before I join my companions."

With evident relief the doctor retreated, leaving her to face the taxi driver's impertinent silver-hued eyes. His mouth curved in an insouciant smile as he started toward the door.

"Gregory should be in the Villa Picasso," he said conversationally. "That's the club's smaller restaurant in the east wing. When you leave here, follow the hallway to your right. It'll get you there without being seen." He paused to look at her, his eyes suffused with the oddly brilliant lights she'd witnessed earlier. She felt an inner quickening. For a sharp, stirring moment, she thought he was going to pick her up again and carry her away. And then he was gone.

Several minutes ticked by before a delayed realization pushed through her dazed senses. How had he known Gregory's whereabouts? Guesswork, she decided, nothing more than clever guesswork. Shaking her head, she forcibly cleared her mind of the distracting cabbie.

At one of the lighted vanity mirrors, she fluffed out her dark hair, checked the clarity of her near-ebony eyes, and added some mascara to the already thick lashes. This is crazy, she thought, backing away from the mirror. She viewed herself critically: not a classically beautiful woman—she didn't kid herself about that anymore. But she had been called attractive, even stunning, and once—an exotic beauty.

"Listen here, Trish McCallister," she warned, "it's going to take more than looks to impress a man of

Gregory's stature. Attractive women are commonplace, a cliché these days. Why should he give you the time of day?" Suddenly all her plans for approaching the gallery owner seemed oafish. "This calls for something absolutely unique," she coached herself, "something that will *make* him take notice. Once he's receptive, you'll tell him about your paintings. He's already Svengalied the careers of several budding artists to enormous success. With any luck—" she sighed, her voice light with anticipation—"you'll be the next."

A quick look around the restaurant told her Gregory wasn't there yet. She slipped into an unoccupied booth, and a waiter approached to offer a menu. She smiled and took it, realizing she might have to order something to stall for time. Deciding against a drink—she needed her wits about her—she perused the menu with considerable alarm. They'd omitted prices and English! The only item she immediately recognized was minestrone. What the heck, she thought, her anxiety building. I'll order a drink. I need the courage.

Sipping a martini, she consulted her watch so frequently she finally lost patience with herself. It's 6:39, Trisha, she scolded fiercely, one minute past 6:38—the last time you checked. Oh, damn, he's not coming. It took me six months to work up the courage to try this crazy stunt, and he doesn't show!

Thirty minutes and a second martini later, she was railing inwardly about the world's injustice. Crime, abject poverty, drugs, she editorialized fervently. A burglary every six minutes, a rape every ten. Civilization's down the drain, she thought grimly.

He's not coming, Trish. He's not coming. Her lower lip began to tremble. The best-laid plans. . . No—no blubbering. Understand? *No tears.* Pack it up, girl. Go back to your nine-to-five administrative assisting, and consider yourself lucky to have a job. No more moonlighting at the easel. Reality has smacked you in the face again, McCallister. You'll never make your living as a painter.

Gathering up her leather tote, she rose, tried to blink away a disconcerting light-headedness and then carefully made her way out of the restaurant and down the long hallway.

Beautifully framed paintings by contemporary artists lined the walls. A sigh slipped out. My work will never hang here, she realized, averting her eyes to focus on the Persian-wool runner.

As she entered the club's elegant lobby, she caught a glimpse of the majordomo flashing by and, startled, momentarily lost her grip on the heavy tote bag. It hit the floor with a sickening thud, and the contents, damp clothes and all, spilled out chaotically. A moan of pure despair escaped her throat. Bending down, tears stinging her eyes, she scrambled to gather up the clutter.

"May I help?" asked a low, mellifluous voice.

"No, thank you," she demurred.

Kneeling, he retrieved a dark object and handed it to her. The gun! Trish stared at it, mortified, willing it to vanish. Then, feeling a surge of defiant bravado, she looked up into the blackest, the most unholy eyes she'd ever seen. *Anton Gregory.*

2

Under the great man's dark observation, Trish's bravado fizzled like a damp match. Unable to speak, and with no idea what she'd say anyway, she took the toy gun from Gregory's elegant hand and stuffed it into her bag. There's no explaining this, McCallister, she warned silently, so don't even try.

"Thanks," she mumbled. Without looking up, she hurried to shovel the rest of her possessions into the tote. Then, using one hand to push herself up from the floor, she awkwardly tried to stand. The tote felt like a lead weight. "Goodness," she breathed, grateful for his steadying hand at her elbow as she straightened, then hoisted the bag up and over her shoulder. Once upright, she realized the room was moving. Spinning, dancing, floating all around her. The carpeting, the walls, even the furniture refused to hold still.

"My God!" She clutched Gregory's arm. "It's an earthquake."

"An earthquake?" He looked faintly confused. "But . . . I don't feel anything."

Uh-oh, McCallister—trouble, she cautioned shakily. She felt herself rocking like a boat in heavy weather, and somewhere in her anesthetized gray matter a still-sober neuron warned her she was dangerously tipsy. Had all that gin rushed straight to her head while she bent over? You never could hold your liquor, Trisha, she scolded herself. A couple of beers at last year's office picnic and they had to call a fire engine to get you down from that tree.

"Can you walk, miss?" Gregory inquired.

"Of course." Silly question.

She took a tentative step, and the room dipped like a carnival ride.

"Hold still," she ordered. A loud hiccup slipped out.

Gregory's eyes blinked twice. "I beg your pardon?"

She squinted at him. "For what?" Strange man, she decided, trying to focus on his face. Why was he shaking his head and looking at her that way?

As Trish stared at him, a nebulous thought nagged her. Something she had to do. Think, she urged. Concentrate. There's something you must do . . . but . . . what? Her mind finally retrieved her mission. Painting? Yes. Tell him . . . what was his name? . . . no matter, tell him about your work.

The man's angular, fine-boned features lifted politely. "Were you leaving? Shall I help you out to your car?"

Car? Silly man. She didn't drive.

By this time Gregory had relieved her of the heavy tote bag, put his arm around her, and was carefully guiding her through the lobby, past the curious whispers and stares of the impeccably dressed polo-playing patrons.

Trisha stared back. As they neared the door, the visibly flustered majordomo rushed up.

Uh-oh, here it comes, McCallister: illegal entry, impersonating a pregnant woman.

25

"Mr. Gregory, my dear man!" he gushed. "Please accept my most profound apologies." He glared at Trisha. "I'll take care of this."

She stopped dead and returned his glare. "What have you done with my baby, you brute?"

His mouth fell open. "Done? Your baby?"

Gregory reiterated her question. "Frederick? What have you done with this lady's baby?"

"Nothing!" he insisted, horrified, his eyes flickering over her stomach. "Perhaps she left it in the ladies' lounge?" He immediately summoned an assistant to find the infant, then whirled in agitation to pick up a ringing telephone.

Trish tugged at Gregory's sleeve. "I think . . . some fresh air?"

He nodded and helped her through the door now held open by the doorman, then assisted her toward the wide brick walkway that bordered the semicircular drive.

She leaned toward him conspiratorially. "There is no baby," she whispered. "But I don't think we should tell Frederick, do you? Poor man—a burnout case if ever I saw one."

Gregory's features crinkled in a frown, then eased in a tolerant smile. "Whatever you say, dear lady." He gently touched her forehead. "Feeling better?"

"Hmmmm?" Trish blinked and hiccuped simultaneously. Wide-eyed, she stared for the second time into the eminent gallery owner's deep, unwavering gaze, but this time she didn't feel frightened at all. In fact, he looked rather sweet. How could she have thought those fascinating eyes unholy?

All at once, she realized the significance of her situation. This kindly gentlemen was Anton Gregory, southern California's career maker—at least in artistic circles—and *she* had his total attention. Mission accomplished! she crowed triumphantly. Your ship's finally come in, even if it won't stop rolling.

"I'm feeling wonderful," she chirped blithely. "I've been looking forward to this meeting for months."

His smile was indulgent, *and,* she decided secretly, just the tiniest bit intrigued.

In the crisp night air, she felt slightly revived but far from sober. An alert drunk, she thought, hiccuping again. The intoxicating scents of moist grass and burning incense wafted past her nose. Burning incense? Perplexed, she sniffed, looked about and then realized it was him. Leaning toward him, she breathed in not incense, but a delicious men's cologne.

"Tartarus." He smiled, amused and indulgent. "Like it?"

"Ummmm." She closed her eyes. "Very much."

"Tartarus," he said, his dark eyes glittering, "is said to be the hottest corner in hell."

"Really?" She sniffed thoughtfully. "It does smell rather like a brush fire."

He cleared his throat. "We seem to have a great deal in common, my dear. You're quite taken with my cologne, and I'm rather fond of handguns and tipsy ladies. Perhaps introductions are in order?"

Delighted, she curtsied unsteadily. "Anton Gregory, meet Patricia McCallister. You may call me Trish."

His eminently dignified expression crumpled in a mirthful smile. Taking her hand, he kissed it lightly, then straightened and nodded. "Trish it is."

"I paint," she announced.

"My." He shook his head as if in wonderment. "I paint too. Could it be a coincidence?"

"Not at all—" she started, then, squinting over his shoulder, thought she saw something. A halo coming toward them? The aura soon materialized, an unsmiling face and body attached. Her taxi driver. Wonder of wonders, the man was absolutley ubiquitous. Maybe he *was* an angel?

"The lady's taxi is ready," the halo announced sternly.

"But the lady isn't," Gregory countered, an unmistakably authoritarian edge to his tone. "We'll call for one when she is, thank you."

It took Trish a moment to realize she was the "lady."

The two men took each other's measure like a pair of rams in rutting season, then each looked at her. Smiling benignly at her taxi driver's glowering face, she inclined her head graciously. "Mr. Gregory will see me home, thank you."

A startled sound escaped the gallery owner's lips. "I'm sorry, Trish, but Mr. Gregory can't do that," he murmured laughingly. "He—or rather I—have a dinner engagement in a few moments. Business—you understand?"

"Of course," she echoed wistfully, "a dinner engagement."

"Will you be all right?" he asked, his fingers stroking her hand.

"She'll be *fine*," the cabbie insisted forcefully. "I'll see her to the cab."

"Thank you." Gregory stepped back, relinquishing Trish gallantly, then reached inside his coat pocket, retrieved a business card and quickly jotted some numbers. "My private phone." He smiled, presenting it to her. "When two people have as much in common as you and I, they must not ignore it. Do you agree?"

"Oh, yes." Trish nodded dizzily.

"Good. Then perhaps you'll show me your work sometime?"

"Anytime," she breathed, impulsively raising up on her toes to press a feathery kiss on his mouth. "Anytime."

Surprise lit his face. "Soon, I hope." As he bent to kiss her hand again, the taxi driver hooked her arm and pulled her out of range.

Gregory quickly unbent. "You will call me, then?"

"Yes—" She felt herself being tugged away. "Yes!" The gallery owner's lean frame had all but disappeared in the darkness as the taxi driver pulled her toward the old green Plymouth. "Yoo-hoo, Mr. Gregory? *When?*" she called out as the cabbie jerked open the taxi's front door, roughly helped her inside and strode around to the driver's side.

"How dare you?" she blurted, the words slurring angrily, as he slid behind the wheel.

"Do you have any idea what you're getting into?" he snapped. "Somebody has to take care of you. You're too damn drunk to take care of yourself."

"Piffle." She felt too good to argue, and if he insisted on being testy, she'd simply ignore him. She slipped Anton Gregory's "private" phone number inside her bra with a shiver of anticipation.

"Where to, lady?" the halo barked.

She gave him her address and then went on to describe the block, the street and the neighbors in minute and gossipy detail. She wound up her spiel with a bright, if tipsy, smile. "Think you can find it?"

He rolled his eyes and started the car. "If I were a real estate agent, I could sell it."

Thirty minutes later, he pulled up in the alley behind her Playa del Rey beach cottage, then walked her around to the beachfront entrance.

"Come in?" she offered, feeling an odd sensation in the pit of her stomach as she looked into his eyes. "I'll make coffee," she explained. "It's the least I can do since you've never charged me a fare." As her mind did a double take on what she'd just said, she cocked her head. "By the way—why haven't you?"

He laughed, flushing slightly. "The truth? No woman's ever undressed in my cab before. I figured if I drove you around enough, you might get the urge again—"

"Down, boy." She smiled, secretly pleased.

Unlocking the front door, she ushered him into the living room and went to the kitchen to prepare the coffee.

"I'm curious," he called to her. "How come a lady who works in Freeway City takes buses and cabs? Where's your car?"

"In Toyota heaven, I suppose," she called back. "A kamikaze moving van took out my little Celica a while back—" She broke off. She'd told the lie so many times she almost believed it now. Putting the coffee on a tray, she joined him in the living room. "Nobody was hurt," she explained quickly at his concerned look, "but my courage suffered. I've been carpooling and busing"—summoning up a silky smile, she handed him a cup—"and relying on the kindness of taxi drivers ever since."

They took their coffee to the front porch, sat on the faded rattan couch and quietly listened to the seductive cadences of ocean waves. Feeling at ease for the first time that day, Trish kicked off her shoes and removed the fake rings and her wristwatch, then settled back on the couch with a sigh.

After a few moments, they began to talk in the way of strangers who've just discovered and feel compelled to know each other. When she told him her name, he promptly nicknamed her Mac. "Trisha," he said, "sounds too much like an ex-president's daughter." She learned his name was Zachary Tanner, that he was twenty-six and had driven a cab for nearly two years, both to pay his way through graduate school and as firsthand research for his thesis on urban crime. At her question about the cardboard boxes, he casually explained that he'd helped a friend move. Almost too casually? she mused. When she mentioned she was older, he guessed her age at "around twenty-eight." She smiled, but didn't correct him. Suppressing a strange desire to tell him everything, she kept her secrets and knew somehow that he had kept his as well.

But mostly she wondered why she couldn't look at him without feeling silly little thrills inside. Why she couldn't stop fantasizing about how it would feel to let her fingers trail down the raised cords of his neck and play in the golden hair that curled into the V neck of his white sweater.

As their exchange of vital statistics lulled, he grew quiet, pensively staring seaward. His face was washed by moonlight, and she found herself studying a pale scar at the base of his jawline, a beguiling imperfection that interrupted his smooth, burnished skin. So her archangel wasn't flawless. Not flawless, but nearly. Well, no wonder, she thought, catching herself, he's a baby still . . . she felt a tiny swell of longing . . . but what a heartbreaker he's going to be when he grows up. . . .

As she continued her dreamy observation, taking in the hard angles and smooth sinuosity of his very male body, a sober awareness cut through, surprising her. Who are you kidding, Trish McCallister? This is no baby, this is no boy. He may be younger than you, but this is a *man*—as fully grown as they get.

The mood abruptly changed. Zach shifted and gave her an intense sidelong appraisal. His fingers made irritating clinking noises on the side of the coffee cup. Studying her, he brushed a hand through his flaxen hair.

"Why are you chasing after Gregory?" he demanded suddenly. "What do you want with him?"

"His influence," she answered too quickly, aware of her defensiveness. "He can make a painter's career."

"For a price."

"What do you mean?"

His eyes flashed like pulsars. "Don't go naïve on me. You know about men like Gregory."

"Of course I know about him. I've spent months searching out his haunts, studying whatever I could learn about his habits."

"Exactly my point. Any woman who goes to that much trouble for a man is prepared to meet his price. Any price. *Anytime.*" The last word mimicked Trish's breathless response to Gregory in front of the Brentmoor.

"So?" she challenged him, a distinct warning in her tone. Was he accusing her of *that* again?

"So," he pushed back. "How does that make you any better than a hooker working Sunset Boulevard?"

The alcohol remaining in her veins ignited as if he'd lit a match to it. She jumped from the couch and paced the porch, halting periodically to glare at him. "The way you look at things, I guess it doesn't." Her voice shook with contained anger. "If I went to bed with Gregory, I'd be a prostitute from Wilshire instead of Sunset, right? No difference save a higher socioeconomic class?" She wanted very much to smack his beatific face. "I've got a flash for you, Zach. You're a prig. You're smug, supercilious, and worst of all, *young*. What do you know about life? About its compromises and trade-offs. About its hard necessities?"

Her anger had the paradoxical effect of calming him. "'Great necessity elevates,'" he quoted evenly. "'Petty necessity casts down.'"

Her jaw went tight. "So what I did was petty?"

"Goethe's words, not mine, Ms. McCallister, but if the shoe fits. . . ."

She snapped back like a rubber band stretched too tight. "My father used to say 'if the shoe fits, deny it,' but I'm not as polite as my father. You and Goethe can take your damn shoe and—" She broke off, struggling against the fury he obviously enjoyed provoking. "How can you presume to know that my necessity isn't great?"

"Is it?" A disbelieving eyebrow raised.

"None of your business!" What enraged her most was his intellectual conceit. The way his smile said, I know exactly what's going on here, lady. He knew *nothing* about her pain, her crises, and yet he spouted quotations and patronized her with his wise old eyes. She stormed into the kitchen and poured herself another cup of coffee. Lighten up, Trish, she counseled herself, he's just a pedantic know-it-all kid. Self-righteous brat! All mouth, no experience. Not a serious threat to a woman your age. No threat at all.

She returned, perched on the railing on the porch's far side and nonchalantly sipped her coffee. Aware that he was studying her, she kept her eyes averted. Just one look at that outrageously smug face might set her off.

"I see you managed to get yourself under control," he observed placidly.

The coffee cup banged down as she glared at his cocksure smile. "Listen." She waved a finger. "You want to see me lose control? Just keep talking." She stood up, temper flaring. "You know *nothing* about my necessities, petty or otherwise, and I don't give a damn what you think of me."

He observed her calmly, then stood up, ambled over and taunted, "If you don't give a damn, why are you shouting?" With a maddening grin, he tapped her nose playfully.

Something in her snapped. Hand poised, she threatened to slap him. When he laughingly blocked the blow, she ducked under his arm, darted to the coffee table and snatched up his car keys. Remembering an old trick from her childhood, she picked up two teaspoons as well and hid them in the deep side-seam pocket of her dress.

With wicked satisfaction she noted his curious expression as she jingled the keys. Once she had his full attention, she raced down the porch steps and ran toward the water.

"Hey, where're you going with my keys?" he yelled.

"Come and see," she called back, issuing a spirited challenge.

She reached the water's edge, whirled around and saw him bounding after her. "Stop right there—!" she ordered.

He halted twenty feet away, his husky frame illuminated by the full moon. Grasping the keys in her left hand, she held them high. "And *stay* there, or your keys go for a swim."

"Damn," he breathed. "You wouldn't?"

Now it was her turn to be cavalier. "Want to talk necessity *now*, Tanner?"

"Mac, quit fooling around and give me back the keys," he warned.

"Hmmm?" She raised an eyebrow, an irreverent smile creasing her lips. "These silly little metal things?" Jangling them, she took another step toward the water. "Heck"—she grinned—"they don't look all that necessary to me—"

As he took a step toward her, she felt a pulse beat in her neck. "*Stay there*, Zach, or they're fish food."

"Those keys are my livelihood," he growled, his eyes glinting.

"Really?" Despite her skittering heart, she shook them and winked. "Get the picture, Zach? Necessity is relative, and if you intend to be the judge of mine, then I'll be the judge of yours. These keys may be important to you, but they don't mean a thing to me."

Grimacing, he took a step forward.

Heart thumping, she took a step backward. "I bet they'll sink like a rock," she bluffed.

He hesitated, considered a moment, then shrugged. "Go ahead and toss 'em," he said indifferently. "I've got another set."

An odd mix of disappointment and disquiet assailed her as he turned away. Had her object lesson about making snap judgments completely fizzled? Her guard down, she sighed and was about to lower her arm when a flash of movement alerted her. Gasping, she side-stepped frantically as he spun and lunged toward her. A second faster than he was, she pulled the spoons from her pocket and threw them as hard as she could. They broke the water with a metallic plop.

With an angry howl, he splashed into the water like a

trained retriever and dove. Seconds later, his head bobbed up for air, and he dove again.

Nervous laughter bubbling, she dropped his keys in her pocket and watched him search. After a few moments more, her elation gave way to guilt. "Zach," she called, deciding to come clean. But his head didn't appear again. Except for the gentle surf, the water was ominously quiet. Time crawled by; how much, she wasn't sure as she scanned the water, wondering why he hadn't surfaced.

Wait—was that a ripple? Or only the flickering interplay of moonlight and shadows? "Zach!" she called, several more times. Why didn't he come up?

There was still no sign of him as she started down the beach following the tidal drift. Of course, she thought, beginning to run, the current had carried him toward the breakwater, a narrow man-made jetty of rocks that traveled out into the ocean several hundred feet. She reassured herself that the water was unusually calm, and he was young and strong—and, please God, a good swimmer?

She jogged the short distance to the rocky seawall and started out, stopping periodically to call his name and search the water. Out beyond the breakers, the ocean was a smooth, flat plane, iced by moonlight. By the time she reached the end of the jetty, she felt the grip of panic. "Zach!" she screamed, straining to see any movement, any sign.

Fear worked at her thoughts and constricted her limbs. "Oh, no," she whimpered, hugging herself. "He couldn't be—" Her imagination conjured images too horrible to contemplate.

Stop it, Trisha—find someone to help. *Move*, she ordered her rigid body. Turning, she managed two shaky steps before she heard the water gurgle. Paralyzed, she felt something catch her ankle. The next instant a body burst up through the water's silver surface.

Spouting water like a towheaded sea creature, Zach locked his hand around her ankle.

"You! You frightened me to death," she scolded him. "I thought, I thought—"

"I used to be a lifeguard," he explained brusquely. "Unfortunately, I missed the class on diving for car keys, so guess what—?" Water streamed over his angry face. "You're going to help me find them."

"Oh." She laughed lightly, reaching in her pocket. "Nothing to worry about—I've got them right here." Intent on soothing his ire, she held the keys out.

"What?" The word blew water in every direction.

"You don't really think I'd throw your keys in the water, do you?" she explained quickly. "It was just a couple of spoons—"

For a moment he was speechless. Then a demonic grin lit his face as he gripped her ankle mercilessly. "Get ready for a swim, Mac." With a snap of thumb and forefinger he sent a spray of water her way. "You're about to join me."

Join him? A crawly sensation raised goosebumps on her skin. Jellyfish, sharks, slimy sea things? "No, thanks," she stated flatly.

A tug at her ankle made her teeter precariously. "Knock it off, Zach," she warned, holding the keys up. "Or this time I will throw them in!"

"Go ahead," he taunted, "and you'll be right behind them."

"Don't be ridiculous!" she argued, desperately fabricating. "I don't swim. And besides, I'm not fond of sharks and . . . scaly things."

"I'm a lifeguard," he reassured her quickly. "And there aren't any sharks here—the water's too damn cold." A vigorous tug sent her teetering forward, arms flailing like a doomed tightrope-walker.

"Stop it!" She jerked her leg back and nearly lost her balance again. "This is a two-hundred-dollar dress!"

He smiled wickedly. "Take it off."

"I'll make you a deal," she blurted. "Your keys for my ankle."

Making a great pretense of deliberating, he finally agreed, pointing to a flat rock next to the one she stood on. "Lay the keys down there."

"After you let go of my ankle."

A grin flashed as he released her.

Get out of his range, she warned herself, stepping back. Watching him, she bent and set the keys on the rock. Before she'd even straightened, he'd swept up the keys, tossed them to a rock beyond her reach and recaptured her ankle.

The grin disappeared. His ice blue eyes were hard. "Take the dress off, Mac."

Anger and fear prickled the flesh on her arms. *"Never."*

"Never?" He snorted. "Suddenly the lady's modest?"

"Let go of my leg." Her voice was low with menace. Why hadn't he drowned?

"Take the dress off or it's fish food."

"You wouldn't."

His eyes sparkled as he lifted her foot and yanked. "On or off, it's up to you." With several frantic hops she managed, just barely, to stay vertical.

"All right, dammit!" She unzipped the dress, pulled it over her head and laid it out on the rocks. In the filmy bra-slip, her bare skin shimmered luminously by moonlight.

"Now the rest."

She glared down at him.

"Take it off." His features gleamed with unnatural lights. "And *maybe* I'll let you go."

Fuming, she slid the straps off her shoulders, then stalled for time by inching the bra down slowly until her full breasts were nearly exposed. Damn you, she castigated him mutely. May the sharks take both your legs. She threatened his glistening form with daggerlike stares and then, trembling, found herself unable to look away.

His eyes caught and reflected moonlight like prisms. Poised in the water like a medieval sorcerer, his face was taut with anticipation as he waited, watching her with brutal singularity. He's positively unearthly, she thought, her breath catching. I musn't let him near me!

"She who hesitates is lost, Mac."

"Wait a minute!" She delayed frantically. "How do I know you'll—" A vigorous jerk stopped her midsentence. Instead of tumbling into the water, she swayed backward and sat down hard on the unforgiving rocks. "Ouch!" she wailed, then grabbed the first loose stone she touched and cracked his knuckles soundly.

A blast of blue words cut the air as he released her and sank into the water, clutching his fist.

Eyes wide, Trish watched him flail about. Intent on escaping, she struggled to her feet, and stepped to the next rock to retrieve her dress. Slippery footing and forward momentum betrayed her. Arms flailing, she hurtled headfirst into the ocean.

The water's icy coldness stunned her. Gasping and sputtering, she felt his hands at her waist. One moment he was behind her, then around and in front of her, his hands sliding over her skin, brushing just under her breasts, hovering dangerously near secret places.

Suddenly a hand spanned her back; another curved around the arch of her neck, and she was pulled toward him, her body coming flush up against a solid, vital force. Struggling to break away, she felt his arms lock around her, felt his lips graze her mouth, then brush across chin, neck, breastbone, each lip-touch lower and more intimate.

"Stop," she gasped, swallowing water. Bubbles foamed and fizzed around them in the turbulence created by her thrashing limbs. What had come over him? Did he intend to drown her? A lifeguard gone bad? She'd free herself from this maniac or go down trying.

Hunching her shoulders, she squirmed down and out of his grasp, then kicked like crazy and swam for the rocks.

"St—stay away from me!" she sputtered, pulling herself up onto the jetty.

He tossed his head back, shaking the dripping blond curls off his forehead. "What kind of thanks is that? I just saved your life."

Ignoring him, she grabbed the dress and keys and ran for the beach. She heard him behind her, gaining. By the time she reached the soft sand in front of the cottage, he'd closed the distance between them. A hand tagged her thigh, and everything went flying as they rolled and tumbled in the sand.

Spent and panting, she lay helpless as he gathered himself up, walked over, then knelt and looked down at her. His silver eyes held her frightened gaze. Hearts still pounding, blood rushing from the chase, they watched each other. Time beat fast and wild as they played out the unspoken ritual of victor and vanquished. His face was victorious. He'd won. The predator hovered over his prey. A ritual as old as time, dominated by drives, by hunger . . . or by mercy? What would he do now? The sand shifted as he bent lower. His hands flanked her shoulders. Night's shadowy, slippery light masked the expression in his eyes, but she didn't need to see it to know his intent. Hot, fast breath met and intermingled as he pressed toward her.

As their lips touched, Trish thought her heart might strangle her with its wild pounding. But his mouth was neither rough nor victorious. As if knowing his power, he teased, coaxed, dared her to respond. Light, tantalizing strokes.

"A remarkable woman," he breathed against her lips, then raised up and looked down at her, his eyes narrowed with desire. "Swims like an eel, runs like a deer. I can't wait to find out what else she does." Then, deliberately, as if expecting a sharp retort, he pressed a finger to her lips. "Truce, okay?"

She nodded, trembling as their body heat accentuated the night's biting chill.

"You're cold." He rose and helped her to her feet.

They walked the short distance to her beach cottage without speaking. Retrieving his keys from the sand and her dangling green dress from a hedge that bordered the porch, Zach followed her inside. In the dense silence of the cottage, she found him a warm blanket to wrap up in, then quickly escaped to her room to shower and change.

A few minutes later and feeling slightly calmer, Trish entered the living room, a white terry robe tightly wrapped and tied around her clean, dry body.

Zach stood by a far wall, huddled in the blanket, admiring one of her seascapes. "Nice." He nodded, then turned and looked her over. "Lookin' good, Mac." He winked at her. "Is the dress gonna pull through?"

"Maybe." She shrugged. "With the help of a very creative dry cleaner. What about your car keys?"

"A little rusty, but safe and sound," he assured her.

As his gaze returned to the painting, she sat down and surveyed him, realizing for the first time that he was soaked all the way from his running shoes up to his blond curls. He looked uncomfortable, adorable, even slightly vulnerable. If only she felt secure enough to tell him about herself; but he was too young, too damn young. He'd never understand. "Zach"—she tried anyway—"sometimes when you want something badly enough, and you can't get it any other way, you have to . . ."

He stiffened and spoke to the wall. "Screw the guy who can get it for you?" His voice slashed through her hopes.

"Damn you!" She despised his simple answers. "Why do you assume I'm going to sleep with Gregory?"

He smirked knowingly. "We both know the answer to that one."

This brash young bully needs to learn his lessons the hard way, she decided impulsively. She turned away, an idea forming. "You must be freezing, Zach. Why don't I rinse out your wet clothes and put them in the dryer? In the meantime you can take a shower." She turned back with an innocent smile.

He nodded hesitantly.

While he showered, she put his freshly rinsed clothing, along with the tennis shoes, into the dryer in the garage and set the timer for thirty minutes. Then she took the black gun from her tote, sat in the living room and waited.

She heard him turn off the shower. "Hey, Mac," he called, "got something I could put on until my clothes are dry?"

"You'll have to make do with a towel."

A moment later, he wandered into the living room, a thick terry towel knotted low on one hip.

"Stop right there," she calmly directed him, the gun pointed at his flaxen-haired chest.

"Wha—" His eyes flashed like quicksilver.

"Drop the towel, Tanner."

"What?"

"You heard me."

"Why?"

"Because I think you need an object lesson, Tanner. How does it feel to be the target instead of the arrow? How do you like being bullied?" She spoke slowly, savoring every word. "Guns are great equalizers, aren't they? People forget all about being self-righteous when they're staring down a barrel—"

"Hey, Mac—come on," he entreated. "You've been watching too many John Wayne movies."

"Drop the towel."

He shifted awkwardly. "I don't think that's a good idea."

"I do. Drop it or I'll blow you away like a piece of lint."

He untucked the towel's edge and let it slide to the ground.

Trish gasped and nearly dropped the gun. He was built like a stallion. An excited stallion. Did the man have no decency?

"Put the towel back on, Tanner, and control your-self!"

He picked up the terry-cloth rectangle and replaced it with a self-conscious shrug. "Sorry, I guess guns turn me on."

"Go get your clothes from the dryer," she ordered. "I'll be right behind you."

"What's the rush?" he appealed, straight-faced, blue eyes wide. "I think I could learn to like being bullied." He quickly raised his hands as she cocked the gun.

"Shut up," she snapped and waved him toward the garage. The gun shook visibly in her hand. She knew young men's hormones worked overtime, but this was ridiculous.

The sight of his lithely muscled body as he dropped the towel again and donned the still-damp clothes all but sent her into the vapors. She'd never had a naked man at gunpoint in her garage before. Or anywhere else, for that matter. His hormones seemed to have calmed down some, and for that she was sincerely grateful, but instinct warned her to send him on his way fast. No telling what else might turn him on. The kitchen stove? The television set?

As he finished buttoning his shirt, she pushed open the garage door. The old Plymouth sat there, parked in the alley, waiting.

"Mac?" he said quietly. "How about a truce? A real one, this time. Maybe if you told me why this Gregory's so important—?"

Let your gun do the talking, Trish, she cautioned herself.

She motioned him toward the car. He took several

steps sideways, hands raised. "Come on, a truce, how 'bout it?" he coaxed. "Cease-fire? . . . Détente? . . . Yield the right-of-way?"

He was shivering slightly. Was he really frightened, she wondered, or just cold from the chill of damp clothing? She felt her heart catch. How lithe and beautiful he was. He could be almost anything, she realized. A thrill spiraled deep in her stomach. An Olympian athlete, a dancer . . . an artist's model. Anything, oh anything, but her *younger lover.*

"He who hesitates is lost, Tanner. Get in that car, drive away and don't look back," she ordered.

3

Zach gunned the old taxi up the on-ramp to the northbound 405 and headed toward Venice and his small second-floor beachside apartment. The freeway's light evening traffic allowed him to drive automatically, rhythmically, allowed his mind to review the day's earlier events. Vivid images captured his consciousness . . . right here in the front seat of this cab, less than an arm's length away, an impetuous, half-naked woman hell-bent to change her clothes . . . then later, her body sprawled on the sand beneath him, a frightened, expectant face, lips wet and salty, hair that smelled of the sea.

Energy surged in the pit of his stomach. Cool it, Zach, he cautioned himself. But despite his efforts, the image of her sparkling black eyes as she held that gun on him stirred his imagination. His fingers stroked the steering wheel, and a sound, half laughter, half awe rumbled in his throat. What a wild woman! The gun quivering in her taut fingers. A face caught between fear and uncertain power, brimming with sexual curiosity. *Drop the towel, Tanner.* Damn, but that was exactly what she'd said! "Whew," he whistled. *"Audacity.* That takes audacity, especially when the gun looks like it's made out of licorice." She'd never know how close he came to taking it away from her and. . . .

Stubborn, feisty female. How old was she? he wondered. In her late twenties? Early thirties? He'd never been with a woman older than he was. Grad school offered plenty of bright, aggressive coeds to satiate body and mind, and if that wasn't enough, the beaches were strewn with well-filled bikinis. But *she* had his blood pumping like no female of any age ever had before. God, but she was incredible.

He took a deep breath and let a fantasy unfold in a slow, sensual haze. . . . His mind saw a tangy, moist plum hanging from a tree, ripening in the sun . . . but not to be picked. Not to be taken until she was heavy with juice and firm of flesh, when her fragile stem gave way and let her fall. He had only to wait for that tender fruit to break loose and drop right into his hands.

A sudden, painful tug deep in his loins made his breath come short. Watch out, man, you're getting carried away. Some instinct warned him he should run the other way, run from her vulnerability, her sharp, sweet desperation. Women like that ensnare men, he lectured himself. With their lush bodies and crazy, wild spirits, they capture a man's imagination. With their bright, sad eyes, they capture his heart. . . .

A freeway sign flashed past him. Washington Boulevard, one and three quarter miles. His exit. He gradually maneuvered the Plymouth into the far right lane. He felt a lightness, a shakiness almost, in his limbs, and the feeling made him grip the wheel tighter as if it were the car that was out of control. Why had it been his cab she'd attached herself to like glue? She'd tumbled into his life with her wet umbrella and fake diamonds, completely naïve to the reality of what she was getting herself into. And why of *all* people did she have to be involved with Anton Gregory? Was she really his type? "Back off, Tanner," he mused aloud. "Things are getting complicated, and this job is tough enough already." Exiting the freeway, he made a left turn and accelerated through a yellow traffic light. A gnawing sensation in his stomach made him wonder if the situation had already gone too far. Could he risk an involvement? No, dammit, he warned himself, not now. *Not with her.*

Trish propped her elbows on the walnut desk-top and rubbed her tired, reddened eyes. It was 9:00 A.M., according to the office wall clock. Brimmer would be calling her into the sales meeting soon, and she wanted to look fresh and alert. Taking a compact from her bag, she studied her drawn features and sighed. She'd slept little the last week. That infernal halo appeared every time she closed her eyes. A soft white aura glowing over Zach Tanner's gracefully masculine body. And those eyes, an oracle's gaze that saw clear to her soul and then judged her for her needs.

A soft yearning enclosed her heart as she felt his hands again, pressing her into the sand, tightening against her shoulders. Arms that could hold her hard, and gentle. It had been so long. His mouth, warm and primitive, threatening. A vibrant body, all force and energy. "Stop it, Trish," she murmured, suddenly frightened at the pleasurable ache that suffused her body.

She exhaled tremulously and pushed away from the desk, then slumped back and let her shoulders rest against the chair's back. A week had slipped by and her taxi driver hadn't returned. Of course, she'd ordered him away at gunpoint—some men might find that an incentive to stay away, but not him. She had sensed even then that it wouldn't stop him. And she realized now that she'd expected him to come back, had counted on it in some unfathomable way.

Her intercom buzzed indifferently. "Ms. McCallister, is the coffee ready yet?"

"I'll bring it right away, Mr. Brimmer."

Trish hung up the phone, stuck out her tongue at it, then hurried to the small coffee room. With four cups filled, one with two added packages of artificial sweetener for Gordon Brimmer, Grover Chemicals' marketing director, she balanced the tray carefully and made her way back to the expansive conference room that adjoined her little cubicle.

"Here we are!" She smiled, bright, nervous, setting steaming cups in front of the two regional sales managers and making sure Brimmer had the one emblazoned "Numero Uno." Taking the fourth cup, she seated herself in a chair at the right of his desk. Each of the three men acknowledged her with an awkward nod. Brimmer cleared his throat. "Ms. McCallister? Was there something else?"

Trish hesitated. Surely he wouldn't? Not again? "Aren't we about to discuss the regional sales campaign? I gave you my input yesterday—the cost-volume-profit projections and the break-even analyses?" She'd spent *days* preparing.

"Ah yes." He picked up a sheaf of papers. "I have them right here." With a thin smile, he cleared his throat again. "Good work—yes, admirable. We'll look these figures over carefully, won't we, gentlemen?" They nodded in unison. "In the meantime, Ms. McCallister, I think Grover Chemicals will be better served by your presence out front. Answering the phones, taking messages, seeing we're not interrupted—that sort of thing?" He hesitated, and she waited for him to clear his throat again. He didn't disappoint her.

Her smile tightened. "But I've instructed the switchboard to pick up the calls."

"No, no, my dear, not the same at all." He rose impatiently, indicating the door with a nod of his head. "You know I prefer the personal touch."

Trish left quietly, quickly, shutting the door behind her with a decided snap.

Seated at her desk, she gave the engraved brass plaque that announced her to the world as Administrative Assistant, Marketing Division, a malicious flick of thumb and forefinger. Two years of concentrated effort to get to this position, and for what? she questioned. A mediocre raise and a twenty-five-cent title. Grover Chemicals must be desperate to clean up their equal opportunity image, she decided sardonically. Why else would they plunk her in a glorified receptionist's job and slap on an impressive title except to boost their quota of "professional women."

Come on, Trish, don't let it get to you, she admonished herself silently. Put in your time, draw your pay. *And call Anton Gregory.* She'd been procrastinating all week, afraid she didn't have any work worthy of showing the great man. But Brimmer had just given her the incentive she needed. Fingers trembling, she drew his card from her bag and dialed his private number.

"Yes?" A bass voice rumbled.

Her heart skittered. "Mr. Gregory, this is Trish McCallister."

He made a sound of recognition. "The Brentmoor? A lovely lady, a gun and—?"

"Yes," she answered quickly, anxious to have that image discarded and replaced with one of a serious, dedicated artist. "You said I might call you sometime—"

"So I did," he concurred. "And as it happens, I'm having a private reception today at the opening of my new gallery in Malibu. Perhaps you'll come as my guest?"

"Oh!" She clutched the phone ecstatically to her breast, then quickly returned it to her ear. "I'd love to!"

"Excellent. See you about two?" he asked, and then gave her the address.

"Two?" She'd need a crafty excuse to leave work

early. "Sounds . . . divine," she trilled. "I'll see you then."

Trish planned her every move, every gesture, every nuance during the taxi drive to Malibu. Life rarely offered second chances, and she would use this one to redeem herself. This time Gregory would see her as she really was—a mature woman, enriched with experience and not a little suffering; an artist who had the potential to capture raw emotion on canvas.

The driver deposited her at a slate stairway that climbed up through jagged black bluffs to Anton's gallery, a cathedral of glass and redwood. As she surveyed the architectural duel between nature and man at his most innovative, anticipation made her feel almost weak.

A limousine pulled alongside the curb, and the uniformed chauffeur let out two dowagers swathed in diamonds and fur. Trish immediately felt underdressed in her burgundy knit tunic and wrap. Fake it, McCallister, she coached herself. Act as if you belong here, and with any luck, everyone will buy it. She acknowledged the grandes dames with a gracious nod, then began a truly regal ascent. So far, so good.

After informing the man at the door of her personal telephone invitation from Gregory, she was ushered into the gallery's spacious and breathtaking main salon. A cantilevered ceiling of pale glass ascended like fragile hands stretching toward the sun. The floor was white marble softened with handwoven silk rugs in muted Oriental motifs. Gauzy natural light sprinkled through the room, illuminating oils and pastels to lucid perfection. Trish shuddered at the aesthetic splendor, unable to move, then felt herself being nudged aside as the two dowagers rustled past her. "Oh, excuse me," she breathed, quite overcome by the room's intrinsic power.

Her eyes were drawn next to the animated, artsy crowd filling the salon. Chatting guests clustered about the walls and easels to view the artwork, leaving the room's center incongruously empty. White-jacketed waiters held their trays of champagne and hors d'oeuvres high and darted through the crowds.

Mmmm, champagne, thought Trish gratefully. That wonderful effervescence, calming and stimulating all at once. But no, no, no, she wouldn't let liquor touch her lips. Not today, this was far too important. Her performance must be genuine and flawless.

She maneuvered through the crowd to a relatively quiet corner vantage point and from there soaked in the ambience for several moments. Finally, as she ventured a step or two further into the activity, an elderly waiter started toward her, the tray of champagne held slightly askew in his arthritic hands. Poor dear man, she thought, shaking her head to discourage him.

He blinked and bowed his head politely, and as he turned away, she saw his foot catch in the tassels of a silk rug. Dear God! she thought, paralyzed, as with a half lunge forward, he caught himself. The long-stemmed crystal danced wildly, champagne slopping over, as he attempted to disengage himself from the rug's tentacles. Why doesn't someone help him? she wondered, looking about. No one seemed concerned or even aware of his plight. Very well, she thought indignantly, I'll help him, and she started toward him. The champagne made tiny puddles on the floor as the glassware emptied itself with his twists. "Just a moment, sir, hold still," she whispered urgently, then stopped herself midstride as he pulled his foot free, turned and walked away as if nothing had happened. She backed away, sighing with relief. Her eyes followed him as he suddenly wheeled and careened straight at her, sliding through droplets of champagne. "Oh, no!" she cried, bracing herself to catch him as he skidded right past her, came to a fully upright stop, brushed himself off and calmly offered the dowagers champagne.

Best get as far away from that man as possible, she decided shrewdly. But her first step carried her right into the slippery path of spilled champagne. Swooping and waving, she teetered, lost her struggle for balance and landed on her bottom. Swearing colorfully under her breath, she rose, teetered forward again and sprawled on all fours. Her bag and wrap flew through the air like missiles. Tempted never to rise, but simply to turn and crawl from the place on her hands and knees, Trish heard a disturbingly familiar voice.

"Ms. McCallister?"

After an interminable moment, she raised her head.

"Somehow"—Gregory smiled down on her in rapt amusement—"I thought it might be you." He shook his head thoughtfully. "Such an affinity for the floor."

The crowd buzzed and began a spirited round of applause as he lifted her to her feet. Gathering up her bag and wrap, he escorted her to his private office and bath, where a maid brought soda water and proceeded to dab the champagne from her tunic. Gregory watched, quietly amused, and resisted all her attempts to apologize. "These wealthy old relics need their batteries charged occasionally," he insisted. "You gave them a jump start. They loved it."

Finally, when the repair work was completed, Trish felt fresh, restored and able—just barely—to brave the gallery's crowd once again. Gregory, silver-haired and resplendent in a black velvet tuxedo, escorted her about personally, introducing her as a dear friend and an artist of great promise. He walked her through salons of fine old art where she quite literally goggled at his private collection of Manets and Gauguins, drinking in Dali's surrealism and Matisse's radiant hues. Then he led her through nimbly lighted displays by contemporary artists and finally to the showroom of his protégés. Stunning seascapes and still-life tableaus in oils and pastels; delirious abstracts, slashes of acrylic color and stark, innovative forms. Dear heaven, she thought silently, my work falls far short of this brilliance.

The afternoon slipped away, and finally he leaned over to whisper, "I'm thoroughly bored by this bunch.

Either you'll have to put on another show to get their hearts going again, or I'm going to spirit you away from here."

Smiling, she inclined her head and winked. "Spirit away."

"Excellent." He laughed and turned her around, pointing her down a corridor toward an exit door. "That way. Quick!"

A moment later they were in his green Ferrari and spinning down Pacific Coast Highway. "My personal studio overlooks the ocean about five miles south of here. I spend a great deal of my time there, working, teaching a few select students. Would you like to see it?"

Was he serious? *"Yes. Very much."*

Once there, he pulled into the driveway and touched off a series of buttons on the dash of his Ferrari. A wall that appeared to be solid rock lifted, revealing a ramp that descended to a subterranean garage. From there, a small elevator took them up to the interior of the house. The living room's decor made Trish's pulse jump. Stark white, black and gray swept the room, accenting geometrically shaped furniture in crimson and art objects in crystal and ebony teak. A wall of glass spanned the horizon. Not a painting in sight, she realized.

"My studio is upstairs." He smiled, gestured and led the way to a tubular extension of the glass wall, a diaphanous half bubble hovering over the ocean below. Inside the tube, a wrought-iron stairway spiraled to the second floor.

Trish climbed the stairway to an elaborate artist's lair. The room was dotted with paintings in progress. A large landscape perched on an oversized easel caught her attention. As she surveyed it, the sound of tinkling laughter came from somewhere in the studio.

"Anton," she started, "did you hear—?" More tinkles of laughter.

Before Gregory could answer, a scantily clad redhead leaped from behind a draped screen and fluttered toward him. "Anton, Anton!" she cried, flinging her downy arms around his neck. "Jacques insists on practicing our pose. I tell him, no, Jacques! I'm tired, my back aches, but he says we must practice holding position if we are to become good artist's models for you. And then, as soon as we achieve position, he . . . well—," she giggled sweetly, seductively, "he—" The rest of her words were garbled as Gregory clamped a hand over her mouth.

Her lilting incoherence turned to something that vaguely resembled French as she deftly unwound herself from Gregory's grasp and danced away, giddy and giggly. Trish couldn't keep herself from gaping at her nearly transparent off-the-shoulder gown.

As Gregory, looking uncharacteristically flustered, turned to Trish, another body appeared from behind the screen. Oh God, thought Trish, gaping at the tall, dark-haired young man, who wore only a towel draped about his middle. This was her second seminude male in a week. An epidemic? Or just dumb luck? She averted her eyes, wishing fervently that Anton would come out of his stupor and do something! Preferably encourage the twosome to put on their clothes.

"Oh—hello there," mumbled the young man, before he darted back behind the screen.

Gregory's voice came out in hoarse and intermittent croaks. "Avril? Jacques? Why are you two still here? I—uh, I dismissed you hours ago."

Dismissed? Surely these weren't his students?

"I know," Avril said, pouting, "but Jacques said we must stay and practice. He's such a perfectionist."

"I see." Gregory nodded, slightly more composed. He managed a weak smile Trish's way. "My models," he explained. "I find Europeans so . . . refreshingly uninhibited." He shooed Avril back behind the screen to dress.

"Your models? You're"—the next words squeaked an octave higher— "painting them?"

Gregory suddenly recovered the full measure of his

self-possession. "Yes, actually, to both questions. They are my models, and yes, I am painting them." The expression on his face said nothing could be more normal, even questioned her consternation. "You are surprised? Or perhaps even shocked? But you call yourself an artist? How can an artist be alarmed at a model's quite-essential state of undress? Unless . . . but surely you've painted a nude?"

She had, years before, and she wasn't about to admit that the nude model's presence had been a major obstacle. She'd never felt comfortable enough to do her best work.

With Gregory impatiently awaiting her answer, she nodded, avoiding details. As his features relaxed, questions tumbled in her mind: Why had his redheaded model thrown her arms around him? And exactly what pose had Jacques and Avril been practicing so faithfully? Instead of asking those questions, she scrambled for some way to smooth out the wrinkles and finally asked politely, "May I see the painting?"

Anton hesitated, considered, then walked to a covered easel and pulled off the cloth with a flourish.

"*Voilà.*" He bowed.

Trisha stared in fascinated disbelief. She angled her head first to one side, then the other. The painting was only half done, and strategic areas were still blank. What exactly . . . my goodness . . . what exactly were they doing . . . ? She suppressed an impulse to ask Anton, partly to avoid appearing hopelessly naïve, but mostly because she didn't want to know.

Anton's voice made her jump. "Conventional morality should never limit creative expression, don't you agree? An artist must be open to life's every pulse." The way he stroked his chin made Trish feel strangely quivery inside. "Well, what do you think of my latest project?" He waited, assessing her intently.

"I think . . ." Looking into his glowing black eyes, she knew she couldn't tell him what she thought if she ever wanted to see him again. "I think I should go home."

"My dear?"

"Suddenly I'm not feeling at all well. A blinding headache. Can't quite focus my eyes. . . ."

To her profound relief he simply nodded. "A migraine. Damnable things plague me constantly." He indicated a plush sectional couch. "Lie down and relax. I'll get you something for the pain. Might put you out for a while—"

Lie down? Put her out? "No." She caught his arm before he'd reached the stairway. "I'll be fine. I have medication at home."

"Home?" He looked disappointed. "Very well, I'll drive you."

"No, no—"

Tinkling laughter floated from behind the screen.

Trish raised a hand. "I wouldn't think of taking you away from your . . . company. I'll take a taxi." Before he could protest, she'd descended the stairway, made short work of the living room and was waiting in the foyer by the front door.

Gregory followed her down, making halfhearted and ineffectual attempts to change her mind. At her insistence, he took a sleek black telephone receiver from the carved wooden box that rested on the foyer table and ordered her a taxi.

As laughter and galloping noises carried down from the studio above, a glimmer of concern tightened Gregory's features. He brushed offhandedly at his tuxedo jacket, then shrugged and smiled. "I don't want to discourage their spontaneity," he explained. "Their ingenuousness makes them a rarity among subjects." A series of startling thuds made the foyer's Chinese vases shake. Trish could have sworn—no, impossible—were they remodeling the house? Reshingling the roof?

Gregory shrugged again. "How is your headache, dear lady?" He smiled, all concern, and started toward her.

"I believe I could use some fresh air," she said weakly. Struggling with the ornate brass knobs, she thrust the double doors open and walked smack into Zachary Tanner.

All three paused, startled. Trish recovered first. "What efficiency!" she exclaimed, relieved. "Mr. Gregory called only *seconds* ago." She stepped closer to Zach's tall frame, resisting a strong impulse to touch him for reassurance.

Gregory put his fists to his waist and regarded Zach suspiciously. "I've just had a state-of-the-art security system installed, young man. No one, not even God, could get through that front gate without setting off the sirens. How did you?"

Zach returned Gregory's glare, his voice packed with hostility. "Nice place you run here. A redhead in a toga jumped off your balcony, opened the gate and took off toward the beach with a guy in a towel right behind her. They disappeared before I could—"

Trish tugged on his arm. Best to get out of here quickly before some disaster occurred. Waving an ambivalent good-bye to Gregory, she maneuvered Zach through the gate and into the timeworn Plymouth. As Zach pulled away, she turned just in time to see a Yellow cab drive up and park. That's odd, she thought. She was about to mention it to Zach when a garbled burst from the dashboard speaker claimed his attention.

Trish's relief at Zach's appearance on the doorstep quickly changed into irritation, then outrage. On the drive home he was cynical almost to the point of slander on the subject of Gregory's ethics, his moral character, even the man's talent. And all because he'd seen two seminaked people running from the artist's front yard. "Models, my foot," he snorted.

Zachary Tanner truly was a prig. She found herself hotly defending Gregory's stand on artistic freedom. "An artist *must* have complete freedom of expression!" she insisted for the fiftieth time. "Conventional morality should never limit artistic expression." The great man's exact words. But, dammit, it *was* true.

"It's not artistic freedom I'm arguing against," Zach insisted. "It's his motives—his, and yours."

"My motives," she stated flatly, "are to get some help with my art career—and at least I'm honest about it. As for his motives, if you mean seduction, Anton Gregory doesn't have to buy women. He's an attractive, charming man." Before Zach could retort, she fired out a question that had bothered her from the first. "Since motives are at issue here, then explain to me, *please,* why you keep turning up like a bad penny every time Gregory and I are together. And don't tell me it's jealousy, because I won't believe that for a minute." She'd like to, but she wouldn't. There was something else going on here.

"Jealousy? My, but aren't we sure of ourselves?" His eyes hovered over her, lightly amused. "Did it ever occur to you that I show up because someone has called for a taxi and I happen to drive one? If you'll think back, Ms. McCallister, I didn't force you into my cab, undress you and take you to the Brentmoor against your will. That was all *your* idea."

Smart-aleck cabbie. She silently gave a litany of thanks as he finally pulled up to her cottage. With a cursory good-bye she let herself out and dashed around to the front of the house. She almost had the door shut when he bounded up onto the porch and stuck a foot in it.

"You owe me eighty-five dollars in unpaid fares."

"What?" She kicked at his foot and tried to force the door shut. "Send me a bill."

With a casual flick of his arm the door banged open, and he glowered down at her. "I haven't had much sleep the last few nights. How about a cup of coffee before I drive home?"

Not much sleep? His halo had kept her awake night after night, too. Maybe . . . ? "Okay, one cup."

As she prepared a doubly strong Haitian blend (he

wouldn't sleep for another week!), she noticed him studying her paintings. Unfortunately, the sight reminded her of Gregory's gallery, and specifically of those paintings by his multi-talented protégés. Even if Anton was still interested in seeing her work, what would she show him? The fruit-bowl still life she'd considered was so embarrassingly typical. She needed something original and powerful.

"Hey," Zach called, pointing to a stormy seascape. "This one's good."

Pleasure warmed her but only briefly displaced her unrest. I wish it were good enough, she thought, diluting his coffee a bit. After all, it wasn't nice to make him lose more sleep, and he did look sort of attractive—scrumptious, actually—posed there in his khaki jeans and pink polo shirt. Posed? The word burned into her brain. My God, she thought, nearly spilling the coffee, a man like Zach would come alive on canvas! She could bring him alive! All that sizzling energy and passion screamed to be painted, to be captured in brush strokes for all time. And what a painting she'd present to Anton.

But the pose, she thought fiercely. It must be completely natural, a pose so authentically Zach that he could maintain it for hours without losing the essential energy that surrounded him like a silvery nimbus. She must catch every subtle nuance. And the scar! Yes, the eye must see his flaws.

Her mind rushed backward, freezing images of him—an excited cabbie driving her to the Brentmoor; a sea demon bursting through the glassy ocean; a victorious predator, panting, waiting, poised above her.

Distracted, she picked up the coffee cup to take a drink and saw her hand shaking violently. Dear God, the effect he had on her. She drew in a deep breath and set the cup down unsteadily. Could she reproduce that effect? Could she recreate raw, untamed life from a palette of color so that other people experienced him the way she did?

Settle down, Trish, she warned, first things first.

Somehow she must get him to agree to pose. Not as easy as it seemed, either. Her heart sank a bit. He despised Gregory, so she musn't reveal the real purpose of the painting. Somehow the necessity for subterfuge bothered her when Zach was the object, especially after all his moralizing about motives. But how could he fault her when he was her inspiration? And if she could reproduce the incredible image that was in her mind, she might ensure that Gregory's interest stayed purely professional. The owner of a string of successful galleries, she surmised, was more businessman than artist, and shrewd businessmen never played fast and loose with the profits. A new and talented artist meant financial gain and critical acclaim for Gregory. Even Zach couldn't fault those motives.

Somehow she knew this painting was an opportunity. An opportunity that loomed vast and wide, its scope beyond her immediate comprehension. She had to do it. The impetus kicked and throbbed within her like a child at term, demanding to be born.

Putting the coffee cups on a rattan tray, she entered the living room. "Zach?" she questioned, her voice soft and slightly tremulous. As he turned, the tray slid from her fingers and clattered to the floor. Without pause, almost without awareness, she stepped over it and approached him. She raised her hand, hesitated, then reached impulsively, letting her unsteady fingers brush over his lips once, twice, then move to explore the small, jagged scar at his jawline. A queer thrill clutched her. "I want to paint you. Zach? Will you pose for me? Now? *Please, don't say no.*"

4

Zach's silvery gaze was an invisible tether connecting them. Wonderment filled her as she stared up into his eyes, into blue-flecked irises that seemed shot through with starbursts. He watched her intently, his mouth parting slightly, his breath coming short and shallow. Time expanded and slowed. He said nothing, eagerly appreciating every smooth curve and recess of her face. His hand came up and covered hers as she caressed his jawline.

His laughter was soft, shaky, not quite in control. "Why me?"

"I can't explain it," she breathed, waiting, wondering if he was about to kiss her, "but it has to be you."

Her heart skipped like a pebble across water as he bent toward her. For a giddy moment she closed her eyes, then opened them briefly to see him still studying her, but closer, just inches away. His warm breath caressed her cheek. "Mac," he murmured, "damn, but you're incredible."

His arms went around her slowly, deliberately, as if he were savoring the silky feel of her, reveling in each contact point as their bodies came together. Stroking her hair, his hand cupped the back of her head and with light pressure guided her up to meet his mouth.

Trish thought she might be dying as sparkling sensations flooded her body. His mouth was stardust, shimmering on her lips. Light and warm and pliant, moving, whispering. She felt a swirling, building excitation as the pressure of his lips deepened and intensified. His arms hardened around her, securing their hold, while strong fingers spanned the back of her head and pressed her toward him.

Breaking the kiss, he nuzzled in the hollow of her throat, murmuring warm, rustling noises as he nipped a vibrant pathway up her neck to her chin and finally rediscovered her parted lips. An undisciplined moan came from deep within him, and then another. His mouth became urgent, hot, a solar flare threatening to burn an incendiary path through her weakening restraint, threatening to consume her in its fiery search.

Inner yearnings soared as she yielded to the pressure of his arms. A hand pressed flat and hard against her shoulder, then moved lower to possess the small of her back, the flare of her hip, sliding still lower, urgently lower, to cup a firm, supple buttock.

With a ragged groan, he pulled her tight against him, every hardened line of his body asserting itself against her soft, suppliant flesh.

Oh, dear God, she thought, making a silent plea, let me find the strength to stop him . . . please . . . please . . . I won't survive this.

Her hands found his shoulders, hesitated, then closed over them with the intent of pushing him away, but, she couldn't . . . she couldn't . . . .

As if sensing her stress, he released her partially, reluctantly, his face flushed and taut with desire, his eyes suffused with need and with stormy conflicts she didn't understand.

"Mac?" he whispered, his fingers playing on the curves of her cheekbones, then feathering lightly across her lashes. Shivering at every change of pressure in his hands, her shaky fingers came up to cover his. Indecision danced in his eyes. His hesitation offered her a thread, a fragile lifeline back to safety. "What are we doing?" she asked huskily, knowing it was a silly question.

He let out a deep breath and his intense expression eased to a bemused smile. "I don't know," he murmured, outlining her lips with exquisite touches, "but you started it. And some brilliant guy once said people should finish what they start."

All her vital parts wanted her to do exactly that. Her body ached and pleaded to let this man sweep her into the swirling force of his passion. It cried to feel the satisfaction of his strength, his weight above her pressing hard against her limbs. Beyond all other needs, she longed to feel him desiring her with his mouth, his hands, his masculinity.

Acutely aware of the insistence with which his thigh pressed against her hipbone, she drew in a long breath and looked up into confusing and tempestuous eyes.

He waited, holding her gaze.

The insidious pleadings of her body almost overwhelmed her with their urgent logic. He's everything, Trish, *everything* your neglected body needs. Let go. *Give in.* Stop protecting yourself and enjoy him. Why not a purely physical relationship? No complications, no heartbreak . . .

Desire and doubt warred within her.

Despite his obvious passion, she sensed a struggle inside him, too, and it triggered new fears and old insecurities. Warnings flashed through her mind. He's young, he's impulsive, he'll make you love him and then leave you for someone his own age. Don't do it again, Trish. Don't let your heart—or worse yet, your physical needs—control you. Back away. Use your head, girl! Back away while you still can.

"Oh Lord," she whispered, pulling away. "I'm sorry. I really am, but I don't think I'm up to the finish you've got in mind."

His eyes clouded with mystification. He hesitated, then shifted awkwardly and half grinned. "Not up to it? Isn't that my—?"

With a tremulous groan, she put a finger to his lips. "Don't say it."

The grin wavered as his lips pressed her fingers. "Okay . . . it was a bad joke anyway."

For a moment she felt reassured, almost safe, and then his features tensed. With a sound of muffled frustration, he pulled her back again, holding her shoulders firmly with his hands and studying her face as if he could find answers there. After several searching moments, a sigh broke from his lips, and he drew her close, holding her tight, almost possessively.

"What is it, Zach?" she questioned.

"Nothing," he whispered harshly. "It's nothing."

But somehow she sensed he'd made a decision . . .

She stepped away and grasped his hand, still experiencing strange surges of energy. "Zach?" For a moment she thought she could feel inner pulses throbbing in his fingertips. She wondered . . . and then knew . . . their hearts were beating in time.

"You called?" he kidded, his voice soft and throaty.

She dropped his hand and stepped back, but even his nearness provoked a hopeless disorientation. Her senses teetered, jumbling judgment and logic. She needed distance to cut the palpable bond between them. Distance to find her own mind again. If she intended to think straight, she had to get away from him. There were things that must be said, must be done.

Turning away, she saw the tray and coffee cups strewn behind her on the floor and gratefully knelt to pick them up.

"No—stay there," she ordered softly as he came to

help her. Without questioning her reasons, he turned to the windows and waited, staring out. She stalled, taking an inordinately long time to gather up the mess, blot the carpet and deposit the remains in the kitchen. Then, feeling calmer, almost detached, she returned to the living room, determined to face him.

Subtle changes in his manner instantly unnerved her. Standing with his legs apart, ever so confident and sure of himself, he flashed a contagious smile. Did that smile say he was sure of her, too? Fighting off an impulse to avert her eyes, she braced herself, then looked up at his brash and handsome face, astutely avoiding the parts that made her feel weak and trembly—his formidable eyes, the tantalizing mouth, the eerie scar.

Where to focus? she worried. Chin? No, not with that gorgeous cleft. Forehead? Uh-uh—those sun-brushed eyebrows. Taking a deep breath, she realized that there was nowhere left to look but his nose. Safety, she sighed, steadying herself. When they weren't flaring, even his nostrils seemed almost innocuous. "Zach, I'm serious about the painting—"

His head shifted—yes? no? a hesitant nod?—and the nostrils moved slightly. Not flaring, she reassured herself, just normal respiration. She wondered if his breath was still warm and male scented. The nostrils moved again, just the slightest quiver. Vaguely aware that her strange preoccupation was a device to distract herself, she suddenly wondered if he might be about to sneeze. She took a hurried sideways step to the end table and, without breaking her fascinated gaze, groped for and found a box of tissues. She offered one to him.

"What's this for?" He took the tissue.

"Just in case," she cautioned him, ignoring his puzzlement. "Now, can we discuss our project? I'd like to start soon—tonight, if possible?" Feeling oddly relieved, she walked over and sank down in the overstuffed plaid couch, then indicated a matching chair across from her.

Still holding the tissue, he hesitated, then sat. "Maybe

you'd better tell me what kind of painting you have in mind."

"Well—" She found it quite easy to look at the whole of him now that they were discussing business. "Oils, I think, and the pose . . . hmmmmm . . . it must flatter, stretch, extend the male form. With natural lighting—" She stood, thinking intently, then walked to the bay window. Gazing out at a black, star-studded canvas with singular concentration, she allowed full rein to the image forming in her mind. Totally absorbed, she saw a crimson dusk riding over the horizon, holding back an indigo sky. Dusk, she thought, feeling an anticipatory shiver that swelled to an inner glow. To catch twilight's fall of light as it played over the contours of his body. "Fabulous," she whispered, "and of course . . . you'll be nude."

"What?" Zach asked. "What did you say?"

She turned to look at him. "Nude."

He nodded thoughtfully. "Sounds chilly."

"Nude at *dusk*."

"Sounds very chilly."

She continued rapidly, caught up in her vision. "I know an isolated section of the coastline south of here. Malaga Cove. There's a two-hundred-foot sheer drop to the beach and just one dirt access-road. No one goes there this time of year—maybe an occasional skin diver, but they won't bother us." She smiled exultantly. "It'll be perfect. Can you meet me there late tomorrow afternoon—in fact, every afternoon until the painting's done?"

She took a step toward him. "Please, Zach. This is so important. I'll pay you model's wages. More, if you want."

Raising his hand to still her, he conceded with a wry smile. "You're a poor credit risk, but I'll put it on your account—along with the taxi fare."

"We'll start tonight!" She ran to her bedroom and came back struggling with an easel and paint box. "Take your clothes off! Quick! We'll work on the pose, and then I'll do some preliminary sketches. I may even be able to get you sketched on canvas, so tomorrow I can start painting."

"Take off my clothes?" He ran his hand nervously through the blond shower of curls. "You sure?"

"Of course." Baffled by his hesitation, she ran back to the bedroom for her sketching paper and Conté crayons. By the time she returned, he had his shirt off. His chest was covered with thick, tangled golden hair that narrowed into a startling and suggestive arrow as it descended over the hard plane of his stomach. Her breath caught as he unsnapped the khaki jeans, exposing another inch of the furry arrow's path.

"Wait," she ordered as the paper slipped from her hand. "I think . . . uh . . . well . . . maybe—" Get hold of yourself, Trish. She exhaled softly, then voiced what she hoped was a rhetorical question. "You do have underwear on?"

He nodded, blue eyes wide and innocent.

"Well—" She scrambled to think of something convincing. "For now, since I'm only sketching and we don't have to worry about details"—she flushed self-consciously and cursed herself for it—"you can leave the underwear on. Yes," she breathed an audible sigh of relief. "Leave it on."

She sat on the couch and busied herself with the sketching material as he removed his jeans. After he cleared his throat for the third time, she reluctantly looked up. He had on stretchy black bikini briefs and nothing, absolutely *nothing*, else. The sight made her wonder if her heart would hold out. "Oh—you're ready." She smiled weakly. "Okay—" Standing, she moved around him as if he were radioactive. "Why don't you stand there." She indicated a spot at the end of the living room some twenty feet from her, which she hoped was a good approximation of the distance and angle she wanted on the beach.

The workings of his long, lean muscles as he strode across the room made her quickly avert her eyes. God, but every flex of that sinewy backside made her stomach grab. This has to stop, Trish, she demanded. If you can't look at the man, how're you going to paint him? She raised her eyes fiercely and saw he was in position, facing her. "Now turn away from me, yes—no, back toward me—no, not that far. Yes, that's it. Hold that." Good girl, she congratulated herself. You handled him just like a pro.

Only the crayon in her hand gave her away. It shook at about nine on the Richter scale. Thank God she had him posed so he couldn't see her straight on.

Hmmm . . . something's wrong, she realized, squinting. The head, the shoulders . . . no, they're not right. What position would achieve the greatest effect? All that latent energy and muscular tension must be conveyed. "Lift your head, Zach." He should be staring into the twilight sun. "Yes, look up. No—" She put her pad and crayon down and went to show him.

"Here," she said, touching his chin lightly until she had him right. Then his shoulders . . . *warm brown skin revealed each shift of muscle, of tendon.* Next, his legs; one should be slightly behind. Her heart nearly lodged in her throat as she imagined touching those long, sturdy legs with their swirls of hair, nearly white from the sun. Curling, teasing, inviting her fingers to play. The swift realization that she was mere inches from his unclothed body made her weak.

She mumbled instructions to the floor.

"Do what?" came his insufferably calm voice. "I can't hear you."

She felt a twist of irritation. If he could control himself, so could she. "I think—" She cleared her throat. "Uh—let's see—move your left leg forward. Yes, there. Hey—leave it there. Stop!" He'd gone much too far. Had he done that on purpose? *Of course*—his eyes would give him away, but she dared not look. "Move it back a bit. There. Stop!" Damn, he'd done it again! He meant to force her to physically reposition his legs. Angrily, she took a breath and prepared to do just that.

As her sensitive fingertips gingerly connected with his thigh, she felt a tingly shock, the kind of electrical snap that comes on a cold, dry day and sends up invisible sparks. Swallowing a squeal, she jerked her hand away.

She stepped back and glared up at him, expecting a silly smirk. Instead, he was straight-faced, unsmiling and sincerely baffled. She searched his face. He *was* doing this on purpose, wasn't he? His eyes would betray him. But they were clear, soft, baby blue. Lord, but this man was crafty and dangerous! He could sell air to the birds.

"Your leg is now too far back," she said shakily, but with as much menace as she could muster. Her whole body now trembled in time with her drawing hand. He must be enjoying every second of this! "Move it forward four—no, exactly four and one-half inches. Yes, yes . . . a little more. There! Leave it *right there!*"

She returned to her chair and collapsed.

Gripping the crayon mercilessly, she made quick, cursory strokes. This would be the damn quickest sketch she'd ever made. Regressing to the geometric shapes she had learned in art school, she used proportionately sized cubes for the head and torso, cylinders for the neck and limbs. With perverse satisfaction, she reduced his splendid body to innocuous circles and rectangles.

As she concentrated on capturing his pelvis in a blocked, sawed-off triangle, she saw him do it. He moved the leg again. "Zach!"

"Sorry," he murmured. "A muscle cramp."

Sure, she thought sardonically. The shifty devil's wasting his talent behind the wheel—he should be selling cars, not driving them.

Observing him, she saw he'd changed position. The pelvis she was sketching now slanted the wrong way. "Move your left foot forward more and put your weight on it," she ordered, feeling a measure of confidence returning. She could handle this. She was an artist.

He fumbled the pose again and again. Finally, with a

tense sigh, she rose, stalked across the room and bodily lifted his leg and placed it where she wanted it. "There." She backed away and inspected him. Now his torso was off. Her fingers spanned his back as she pressed him slightly forward. "Better, umm hmmm, that's close," she mumbled. Coming around in front of him, she crouched and placed a hand on each sleek hipbone to bring him forward and around just a fraction more.

All at once, she realized she was staring into a furry belly button. His stomach was flat and tight. Pelvic muscles, with their arrow of golden hair, shifted and tensed right beneath her outstretched thumbs. Oh my God, she moaned silently. What am I doing here? She stared at her thumbs as they nestled wantonly in his flaxen down, and her pale, quivery fingers stretched over the tanned rise of his hips. The black bikini was level, flush with her face. Suddenly she couldn't breathe.

With a strangled gasp, she straightened, taking her hands off him as if she'd touched a live wire. This will never work, she cried silently. The painful excitement he evoked, the very excitement she hoped would blast forth from the painting, made it impossible for her to touch him, even to be near him. "Zach." Her voice made raspy sounds as she returned to the couch. "Let's quit for now."

He broke the pose and faced her. "Why?"

She hesitated, afraid to admit her vulnerability. "Well, for one thing, you won't hold the pose," she snapped, covering her own weakness. "I can't stop my work constantly to coach you back into position. I'd never get the painting done."

"That's easily solved—"

Good grief, did the man have an answer for *every-thing*?

"I'll hold still. Here—" He shifted back into the pose and maintained it perfectly. "Nothing to it." He grinned, moving only his mouth. "A regular statue. When you're done with me, you can donate me to the park commission."

She smiled in spite of herself. So—he had been baiting her earlier. "Zach—it's late. Maybe you'd better go home."

"Impossible." He grimaced. "My body is fused in this position. Quick, paint me."

"No—no more tonight." Why did she feel like a mother talking to her child? Trish, he's *too* young.

He conceded reluctantly, stretched like a jungle cat, relaxed and moved to the chair his clothes lay on. It didn't seem to bother him in the slightest that he wore almost nothing. He seemed oddly unconcerned, almost unaware of his physical appeal.

"What time tomorrow?" he asked, pulling on his jeans.

Tomorrow? How did she tell him that just being close to him suddenly frightened the daylights out of her? His youth, his intensity. Their sparring didn't feel like fun and games anymore. It felt like winner take all, and she'd lost too many times before. How did she tell him that his barely contained passion frightened her only slightly less than her own?

"I'm . . . not sure I want to go on with this."

Crossing his arms on his chest, he looked at her hard. "Why not?" The determination in his eyes surprised her.

The painting got me into this, she thought, a trifle irrationally. The painting will get me out. "An artist has to feel . . . ready," she argued impulsively. "I'm not sure about this painting yet. I have to . . . think." She faked a casual shrug. "Why start a painting I can't finish—right? Your brilliant friend, remember?"

He came over to her. Kneeling, he lifted her chin and looked full into her confused dark eyes. "What's bothering you, Mac? If it's me, I can promise you right here and now that I won't cause any problems. I'll pose on my head if you want me to. I'm not sure why this painting's so important to you, but since it is, I'll do whatever I can."

He waited, watching her.

Why did she now feel like the child to his father?

"Okay," she agreed finally, his gentleness melting her indecision. "But two conditions—"

"Anything." He smiled, caressing her chin.

"Do you have flesh-colored bikinis?"

"What?" He laughed. "I'll run right out and buy some."

"Good, that way you won't have to pose completely nude."

"Hey—I don't mind."

I do, she thought desperately, very much. "It's just a precaution in case someone decides to take a walk on the beach. We don't want to get arrested."

He smiled, vaguely wicked. "But how're you going to paint my—"

She flushed. "I have an incredible memory."

"What's the second condition?"

"We maintain a strictly business relationship until the painting's finished. You're the model; I'm the artist."

He drew his hand away from her face, stood and very deliberately recrossed his arms. "And once it's done?"

The way he looked at her made her pulse rush. "I don't know. We'll find out . . . then."

"Okay—you've got a deal." He retrieved his shirt from the back of the chair, pulled it on and moved toward the front door to leave. "When do we start?"

"Tomorrow? Can you pick me up at the Great Western Bank Building, say four-thirty?"

With a nod, he was gone.

Before falling asleep that night, she lectured herself severely. All the old, familiar themes about using her head, about not letting her heart or her body run rampant, stampeding over reason and restraint; and on a more practical level, about not blowing this once-in-a-lifetime opportunity to have an art career, an honest-to-goodness art career! By the time she fell asleep, she'd quelled the gnawing fears and built a steely fortress of willpower around her errant physical urges.

Each passing day, Trish's painting came closer to completion and her fortress came closer to crumbling.

By the close of the fifth sunset at Malaga Cove, the painting needed only finishing touches. The fortress needed major repairs.

Zach stood posed on a jutting formation of rocks while white surf bubbled and boiled around the granite pedestal. His body was illuminated by an aura of apricot light. Observing him, Trish felt the double-edged conflict that had been at her for days. The woman in her saw a frighteningly sensual male; the artist saw a body that demanded contrast to give expression to its energy. Contrast.

As the sun hung over the horizon like an orange fireball, she suddenly saw the answer to the artist's problem. "Zach, turn toward me a little more. Yes! Look to the right of the sun." A fractional shift, but the effect was magnificent. That's it, she thought triumphantly. The fire now caressed two-thirds of his body, while the remaining third was concealed in near darkness. Ominously defined by shadows, her angel had a dark side. She hurriedly mixed colors to varying hues, and then, using careful brushstrokes, created the shading effect.

Dropping her brush on the palette, she stepped back to see. It *was* magnificent. "Zach, it's done!"

When he didn't answer, she looked up.

He hadn't moved from the pose. Hadn't he heard her? As if transfixed, he stared past the sun like a glowing alien. A shiver traveled her spine and left her chilled. He looked preternatural, a shining mystic. Her gaze traveled down his body and then froze midway. What—? Tensing, she strained to see.

A mark traced the right side of his stomach, rising just above the band of his briefs. A series of tiny fissures drew a jagged path in the burnished skin. A scar! She knew instantly. Much like the one on his jaw, but longer, more explicit. How had she missed it before? Why did she see it *now?* The changed angle of light? The sudden chill in the ocean breeze?

With one long stride, she caught up the palette and mixed colors to a pale flesh tone. Using feathery brushstrokes, she recreated what she saw. But the briefs . . . the briefs he wore blocked the scar's crooked descent. She hesitated, her fingers tightening, pressing white against the brush's slender handle. What was its path? How far down did it go? Authenticity seemed vital. "Zach?"

Unmoving, his eyes blank, he viewed the horizon.

"Zach! The scar on your stomach—"

A shadow crossed his face as he turned to her. His eyes shone, a glassy reflection of sun-glazed water. As though knowing her reasons, he bent, slipped off the briefs and let them drop into the ocean surf that swirled around the rock he stood on.

A painful thrill broke deep within her. Her hand vibrated. She could barely control the brush. The scar dipped down and disappeared in the hollow of his pelvis. Her uncontrolled strokes enhanced its cruel unevenness. Within minutes, emotionally depleted and exhausted, she finished. The brush slipped from her fingers and clattered on the flat rocks under her three-legged stool.

With a deep, shuddering sigh, she bent forward, cradling her head in her hands. Her heart slammed against her ribs. What's happening to me? Oh, please, don't let me feel this way. Not again. *I don't want to feel this way.*

She felt his hand on her arm, and shook her head. If only he'd just go away. . . .

When she raised her head, he was pulling on his jeans and shirt. She inhaled deeply, steadied herself, then began to clean brushes and palette busily, throwing them in her paint box. By the time she finished, he'd carried the wet painting the short distance to the access road where the car was parked and had carefully propped it up in the backseat. It took one more trip to gather up the portable chair, paint box and easel. Working fast, they packed the equipment in the trunk.

Once in the car, she sat as close to her door as possible.

He started the Plymouth's rickety engine, then looked over at her, his eyes mixed with laughter, pain and a storm of other undiscernible emotions. "If the car had a running board, you could ride shotgun, but since it doesn't, and since that door *isn't* reliable, I suggest you lock it and move this way. Sitting closer to me couldn't hurt as much as colliding headfirst with the asphalt."

He's right, of course, she thought. Locking the door, she slid a bare two inches to her left.

He shook his head as if she were hopeless, sighed, and began a bumpy ascent up the access road. If only he knew how much she wanted to discard her fears and slide next to him. Her senses worked fervently against the fortress. She imagined her fingertips twining through the golden hair on his chest, rustling through the windblown mane that framed his stormy face. An image of him standing naked on the rocks flashed through her mind; she saw a vivid, whitened scar threading toward his groin.

Her body went rigid as she felt an inner shower of blissful stimulation and then a painful wrench deep in her stomach. And suddenly the sensations became more intense, more powerful than ever before.

Sensing her turmoil, he looked over at her, his face harsh with its own torment. His eyes were whirlpools of sensual needs. They caught her, held her with their volatile plea. All at once she knew, beyond restraint or fear, that she wanted him, that she had to have him.

5

Zach gripped the steering wheel hard enough to bend it. The gesture allowed an illusion of control, but he couldn't kid himself. He was close to the breaking point.

His peripheral vision told him she was still crammed against the car door as if terrified he might molest her. Perceptive woman. But at the same time she seemed to be studying him, and when he'd glanced at her a moment ago, her expression had exuded a sexual intensity so pure it made his stomach twist. Was he going crazy? The signals she sent were so contradictory he felt paralyzed. Damn, he'd never wanted a woman this badly in his life!

Abruptly braking at the next intersection, he frowned at the street sign. Via Arroyo? Where were they? Had he missed the turnoff? He *was* going crazy. Paseo del Mar, Paseo de Oro—they all sounded the same. How the hell did you drive in Palos Verdes without an interpreter?

If she looked at him that way much longer—an ache, sharp with pleasure, coiled within him. If she looked at him that way much longer, something was going to happen.

As he continued down the narrowing street, the sun dropped into the ocean and a silvery new moon took command of the sky. Darkness crept over the deserted road.

He strained to read street signs. For some stupid reason he didn't want Mac to know he was lost. They passed a school yard on the right, and he knew he'd gone too far. Negotiating an illegal U-turn, he started back, then heard her shift in the seat. His head turned sharply. Was she sliding closer? Her black eyes shone. Like onyx stones, they deflected the thin moonlight. Her lips parted in anticipation.

His breath caught. He turned the car toward the curb. Too sharply, he realized too late. The car veered right, hopped the curb and rode the rocky embankment until he could bring it to a stop. Christ, he thought, shaking violently. Twenty feet more and they would have gone over the side and hurtled two hundred feet to the beach.

He flung the car door open and strode toward the cliffs, stopping ten feet short of the edge. The moon was a broken ribbon mirrored on the ocean's still surface. He crossed his arms, hugged himself and tried to stop shaking. He'd almost killed them both.

The plaintive cry of seagulls cut the air.

A car door slammed. He turned and saw her coming toward him. Her eyes were wide and luminous. Her lips trembled. She looked like a fragile, frightened doe. Beautiful, incredibly desirable. A moan locked in his throat. Excitement surged through his loins.

As she reached him and looked up, the uncertainty in her eyes made him want to sweep her up and cradle her in his arms. He would hold her, protect her, kiss the fears away. Nothing would ever hurt her again. "Mac," he said in a low, shivery growl.

His stomach muscles tightened as her fingers touched his face, trembled along his jawline. Soft, full breasts bobbed against him as she rose up on her tiptoes, hesitated, then looked up into his eyes and placed a whispery kiss on his lips.

I want you, I want you. . . . Was that what she'd murmured? His moan sounded deep and throaty as he pulled her close with a single encompassing sweep of his arms. For a breathless moment he held her, felt her heart skitter wildly against his chest, heard his own heartbeat roar in his ears. I have to have this woman, he thought. *Now.* I can't wait any longer. His body responded swiftly, mindlessly. Energy pulsed into his loins.

He heard a sweet sound, almost a whimper, come from her as she entwined her arms around his neck. The sound made his heart hurt, and he kissed her fervently, hungrily. The urgency of his need compelled him, the ferocity frightened him. He had to have her. He must not hurt her.

She broke the pounding kiss. "Zach," she whispered against his lips. "My house. Let's go there."

He couldn't hold out that long. Her house might be in China. He'd never make it.

Letting his hands glide over her back, climbing and falling with every delicate curve, he fought against the urge to pull her down onto the grass and ravish her. Her breasts felt cloud soft against his chest. His hands ached at the thought of touching them. But somehow he had to get to her house, he told himself fiercely. Not here. Take her home.

Pressing kisses on her closed eyelids, her nose, her unsteady chin, he picked her up and carried her to the car. In his excited state, every step brought a vivid reminder of desire.

Her fingers played through his curly hair. She was a sensual child, utterly abandoned, discovering a mesmerizing new toy, murmuring excitedly, breathily. Her hand slipped underneath his knit shirt to stroke him and feather through the curls that matted his chest. The fire in her eyes stirred him beyond reason. *He couldn't wait.*

He reached the car, set her down, jerked open the back door and lifted the painting out. With one continuous motion, he propped it against the car's fender, picked her up, laid her down on the backseat and slid in next to her.

"Zach?" Her hands flattened against his chest, holding him back with the shaky question.

A groan shook him. "Mac—remember Goethe? I'm sorry, I'd like to take you home, but we're talking necessity here, *great necessity.*"

An ardent smile flashed over her mouth. A whimper came from her throat again as she rose up to meet his lips. Her surrender made his passion flare. Pulling her up to him, he kissed her hungrily, then laid her back on the seat again. His hands shook as he worked open the buttons of her blouse. Finally, unable to quell the impulse, he slid a hand inside her blouse to cup one of the soft ovals as he undid the remaining buttons.

The velvety breast trembled in his hand. Oh God, the feel of her tore him apart.

He heard her breath catch. With a choking sound, she rose to help him, hurriedly working free the last buttons. She pulled the blouse off, and he sucked in air at the sight of her. Straining in the confined area of the car, he tugged his shirt off over his head, then stopped himself long enough to look at her dark, lush beauty. His pulse pounded as her silky breasts flattened against his chest. Oh God, she felt good. He held her tight, crushing her naked skin and swollen breasts against him.

His heart pounded, while hers thumped wildly, out of time, in time. A dance of frenzied beats.

Finally, breaking apart, they continued to undress silently. Tense with expectation, neither spoke. Their rushing breath filled the old taxi with sound and filmed the windows with steam. Gauzy moonlight filtered through the haze and sprinkled the car's interior with phosphorescence.

Trish lay naked on the seat, tight thrills coursing through her body as she watched Zach pull off his jeans. Shadowy light enveloped him. Muscles tensed and flexed as he worked in the limited space; the hair on his tanned body glistened like finespun silver.

He turned to her, naked, and her heart beat so hard she was afraid it would burst through her chest. As he lowered his body alongside hers, she felt his hardness press aggressively into her thigh. Sparks crackled where he touched her.

"Mac," he whispered harshly, "I've never needed a woman like I need you."

She felt herself go rigid and then quivery as his hand took her breast in a fierce, impassioned caress before it stroked down her side, palmed one firm buttock and pulled her hard against him. His sleek hardness pressed deep into the soft flesh of her belly. Sharp spurs of desire burned within her; a hidden core of femininity throbbed and pulsed.

Releasing her, his hand slid over her hip, into the hollow of her pelvis and down to the vee between her legs. Trish felt currents of pure pleasure as his fingers tantalized her inner thighs. Suddenly their teasing was serious. His breathing was hot and rushed as he touched and explored dangerously near her most intimate parts. She tensed as he probed and entered warm, wet recesses. Knots of sharp, sweet pressure caught in her stomach. "Zach," she moaned, then reached down as if to stop him, but couldn't. The highly charged source radiated fierce pangs of pleasure as his fingers stroked within her. Trish felt a frenzied excitement climb her body.

If he didn't stop, he would drive her crazy with desire. Did he mean to make her scream his name and beg him to make love to her?

Moans of wanton joy broke from her throat as he

continued mercilessly. Her body tensed frantically, rocking, undulating with needs that had been denied for too long. "Oh God, Zach, no more," she whispered harshly. A silent cry strangled the words forming on her lips. "I need you—please—"

With a savage, broken moan, he withdrew the seductive fingers and took her mouth with his. A knee pushed between her legs, separating them as he lifted his weight above her. Trish felt his taut maleness press into her thigh in its electrifying search for her warm depths.

Pulsing desire made her arch her back and strain toward his nearing thrusts. And then he found her. Their cries slashed the air as he entered, pressing into her with unchecked passion. His urgent movements stung and thrilled and filled her body with soaring fires. She needed this, needed him with a fervor that overwhelmed and possessed every cell, every fiber of her body.

A groan ripped through his clenched teeth as he lifted her hips and buried himself deep inside her. Trish felt a soaring riot of chaotic sensations. Barely able to breathe, she held him fiercely, possessively, feeling the muscles of his back work and tremble beneath her fingers. The wild, wonderful joining of their bodies left her gasping, giddy, near delirious. Suffused in rapture, she felt a brilliant inner glow and surrendered to it wholly. Her body responded with abandon, eagerly, so eagerly as he moved lustily, forcefully within her.

His ardent thrusting slowed, became deep and good and powerfully rhythmic as he raised his head to look at her. "You're beautiful," he whispered hoarsely, "incredible . . . fantastic." Her heart pounded wildly as he hesitated, then began again with slow, deliberate strokes. She saw the rigid strain in his features as he fought for control and felt him slow even more, until finally he stilled. Quivering like tensile steel, he was lodged deep inside her. "Tell me you want me, Mac," he breathed roughly, brushing her face with hurried kisses. "Oh God, tell me. I need to hear you say it."

"I do—" she cried spontaneously, her fingernails digging into taut flanks. She'd never wanted anything so badly in her life!

"Tell me, show me," he rumbled, his voice catching tremulously.

Her fingers contracted against the rise of his hipbones, and she moved against him in tiny, tight lunges. His face constricted with sharp, urgent anguish as he fought for control, fought against surrender to her seductive, enveloping heat.

"I want you, Zach," she breathed fiercely. "Love me—" her voice broke with passion, *"love me."*

With a shuddering groan, he pressed into her and then, unable to stop, thrust again, totally lost to the driving impetus of his need. Desire surged and pounded into him until he was moving, stroking, filling her again and again.

Their strident, sensuous sounds mingled, rocketing their shared excitement to turbulent heights. Trish felt pleasure so exquisite it pained and thrilled and devoured her. His slightest movement tingled and reverberated inside her with violent, ecstatic shimmers. She was lost in bliss, lost in the joy his sweet, hard body gave her. Lost as he fed her with ardent strokes, thrilled her beyond dreams, and carried her spiraling up and over the edge. "Zach!" she cried, as swelling waves broke and pounded through her.

His arms closed around her, lifting her, crushing her to him as a brutal moan shuddered through his body. Another spasm racked him, and he cried her name. Finally his body quieted and he held her gently, tightly, pressing whispery kisses and incoherent murmurs against her throat, her cheeks, her closed eyelids.

Cradled languidly in his arms, Trish felt swells of warm enchantment rock her. "Oh, Zach," she breathed, feeling a frightening need to whisper endearments and talk of love. "You were wonderful," she said instead, then echoed his own words. "Incredible, fantastic."

Their bodies still joined, they lay limp and spent, feeling the little, shivery aftershocks of love. He touched and kissed her lightly, tenderly, telling her over and over what an incredible woman she was. His silver eyes glowed. She suppressed a compelling urge to caress his face, to heal the scar with her fingers, to confess her turbulent feelings for him. A tiny remnant of reasoning insinuated itself into her reverie. Be careful, Trish, it whispered. Go slowly with your love. She listened halfheartedly and then, unable to completely deter the swell of emotion, she ruffled his flaxen hair, twined her arms around his neck and kissed him lightly on the chin.

He sighed, kissed her back and studied her affectionately. A space of tender quiet passed until finally he withdrew from her slowly, reluctantly. With careful agility he pushed himself upright and sat on the edge of the seat, next to her waist. His mouth curved in a charming, unsteady smile as he playfully tapped the tip of her nose. "You're not a bad little artist, either."

She laughed and almost told him if it was vocation he wanted to talk about, his driving skills could use some attention. Instead, she sighed and stretched and propped her feet up on the seat back. Heavens, she mused silently, isn't life utterly wonderful.

Sitting up with the idea of hugging him and holding him and smothering him with kisses, she dreamily decided against such an energetic feat and rested her chin on his shoulder instead. As she gazed out the car's moist windows, a slow realization dawned. They were in Palos Verdes. In a car. On an embankment near the edge of a cliff—a public road a few feet away! That last part worried her the most. "Zach," she gasped, straightening, "we've got to get dressed. This area is well policed. If they catch us—"

Headlights loomed behind them as if to prove her statement true. Zach found his jeans and hastily pulled them on. "Stay in the car," he ordered, getting out. "I'll handle this."

Trish fumbled desperately with her clothes. Forgetting

underwear, she slipped her cotton slacks and plaid blouse on over bare skin. A Volkswagen Rabbit sailed by without stopping. She let out a deep sigh as Zach opened the door and stuck his blond head in. An irresistible grin crinkled his face. "Told you I'd handle it."

Helping her out of the backseat, he lifted the painting from where he'd propped it against the car fender. With a thoughtful frown, he held the canvas away, squinted at it in the dim light and then repositioned it on the backseat. "Do I really look like that?" he wondered aloud.

She nodded. "Better." *Much better.*

An obvious beam of pleasure lit his face. He gave the picture a second glance. "No wonder you couldn't keep your hands off me." He reached for her, but she swatted his hand away and ran around to the passenger side. When he got in, she slid next to him and let her fingers run up and down his thigh.

His eyes darkened; he cleared his throat.

"Let's go to my place and do it in bed," she whispered. "Properly."

He smiled. "Let's stay here and do it in the backseat again. Improperly."

Staring up at his handsome face, at the subtly cleft chin and the full, parted mouth, she felt the silly little thrills again, the same schoolgirl butterflies she'd had the first night they met. He was still lithe and beautiful . . . and still too young.

Another pair of headlights interrupted them. The car slowed, then went on.

"I'd better take you home," he murmured. "I think they're on to us." Ignoring the scatter of static that came from the taxi's microphone, Zach glanced at his watch, then turned the ignition key.

She straightened reluctantly, not quite ready to give up the thrill of more lovemaking in the backseat. "Okay," she agreed finally.

"Two conditions," he asserted, much to her surprise.

"If you want to get home safely, stay on your own side—over there." He pointed to the far side of the seat. "And keep your sensuous little fingers off my body. Otherwise, I may run us into a bus."

About to protest, she saw from the set of his face that he was completely serious. "Chicken," she taunted softly, sliding over to her side.

Once at her beach cottage, he carried her inside, stood her upright in the middle of the living-room floor, then went back for the painting.

"Put it there," she directed him as he returned, pointing to a carved wooden easel next to the couch.

He positioned the painting. "How's that?"

"Hmm," she observed, considering. But he gave her no time to contemplate her work. Sweeping her up in his arms, he kissed her until she couldn't breathe. "Help," she sputtered, gasping and laughing as he released her.

His warm, moist lips pressed the sensitive curve between her nose and upper lip, then smoothed over an eyebrow. "I'd love to help you," he murmured, "but due to circumstances beyond my control—" He sighed regretfully. "I have to leave."

She stepped back, out of his arms. "Leave? I thought you were going to stay?" Her voice was pouty, and the disturbing possessiveness she felt surprised her.

"I can't, Mac," he apologized. "It's late. There's something I have to do."

Her possessiveness was joined by suspicion and gnawing doubt. Late? It wasn't that late. Where was he going at—she checked the wall clock—eight-thirty? And to whom? Her stomach twisted. Then she caught herself. Why was she questioning him? What gave her the right to know his plans or to second-guess his motives? If he wanted to leave now and never come back, he had the perfect right. He owed her nothing. She owed him nothing . . . except eighty-five dollars in cab fare and an unspecified amount in model's fees. Anyway, she didn't care what he did. Shouldn't care.

"Sorry, the noble profession calls." He shrugged. "We taxi drivers never sleep." Lifting her chin, he kissed her oh so temptingly. Her heart thumped as his lips lingered. Maybe he would stay?

With a light kiss on her nose, he was gone.

Gone without a word about when he'd be back. *If* he'd be back. Without even saying he'd call.

"Oh, Trish," she moaned to the ceiling.

Shuffling dejectedly out to the front porch, she sank down in the rattan couch. Her fingers touched lips that still vibrated from the pressure of his kiss. With a shaky sigh, she pulled her legs up and hugged them to her. "Okay, lady, he may be the best thing that ever happened to you, but come on, he's *twenty-six*. A veritable boy in a man's body."

She let go of her legs and sank back. Oh, but what a body. And what a shamelessly potent man he was. The memory of his fierce love made her senses swim and her limbs go weak. "Trisha, my girl," she sighed, "you're in deep trouble."

Balancing the coffee tray expertly on one out-stretched palm, Trish tapped on Gordon Brimmer's door.

"Come in," he harrumphed.

"Good morning," she offered pleasantly, setting his cup on the coaster next to a hairy-knuckled hand that hesitantly touched out numbers on a desk-sized computer.

She waited a moment nervously, and when he didn't look up, said, "Excuse me, Mr. Brimmer, but I'll need the sales volume data in order to prepare the reports in time for the next meeting."

"Hmmph, I'll never get used to this damn machine." He switched the computer off and looked up at Trish as if it were her fault. "What? What is it you want?"

"I need the sales volume numbers for this month."

"Why?"

Was Brimmer's brain going soft along with his body?

"To prepare the statistics for the next staff meeting, as I do every month."

"Oh." He hesitated, harrumphed again. "No need to worry about that anymore, Ms. McCallister. Willoughby's girl will be preparing those reports from now on."

Willoughby's girl? Willoughby was the new assistant director of marketing. When had they hired him a "girl"? Probably made darn sure they found someone willing to put up and shut up. A "girl" who wouldn't make waves. "Why the change in procedure?" she asked evenly.

"Well," he explained, "since the regional sales data is now being directed to Willoughby's office for his analysis and perusal, it's simply more efficient for his girl to generate the reports and then submit them to us." He settled back in his chair, looking quite pleased with himself. "Takes a load off my hands, I can tell you." He smiled at her, a hint of apology in his jowly face. "And yours too, of course."

He had just usurped her only area of responsibility. What was she to do now? Dust desks? Water plants? "Mr. Brimmer, I don't need a load taken off my hands. I'd like more responsibility, not less."

The apology vanished. "The procedural change was an executive decision, Ms. McCallister. Not yours to question, or mine." He picked up the coffee cup, paused before taking a drink, then looked at her and smiled with appalling sincerity. "You're a bright woman. I'm confident you'll find ways to keep busy."

Her mouth dropped open, then clamped shut, biting back a retort. She wheeled around, clicked out of the office, dropped the coffee tray in the wastebasket and walked straight to the elevator. Thumbing the down button, she made her plans. She'd go straight to George Lawson, the personnel officer, and arrange a transfer. Her stomach twisted nervously. Yes, dammit, she'd transfer to another division.

She exited the elevator two floors lower. Lawson's congenial secretary greeted her, then buzzed the personnel officer and announced that Trish McCallister was waiting.

"Come on in, Trish," Lawson called through the partially open office door. She felt a flash of relief at his amiable voice.

Even before taking a chair in his small office cubicle, she blurted out her plans.

The sandy-haired young man listened carefully, then looked disturbingly grave. "You know the risk you're taking, don't you, Trish? Once you've formally put in for a transfer, Brimmer has to be notified—he then has the option of filling that position immediately."

"Immediately? Before I've found another position?"

Lawson nodded, unsmiling. "You've got the picture."

"Where does that leave me?"

"Out of a job, I'm afraid."

Suddenly she felt hopelessly entrapped. A twist of paranoia penetrated her thoughts. Did this whole company have some kind of conspiracy against her?

"Nevertheless, I'm going to transfer, George. I'll take my chances."

The remainder of the day was equally disturbing. Brimmer called her in and expressed shock that she should want to leave Marketing. Then, without the slightest show of interest in her reasons, he made some vague remarks about her decision to "toss aside a perfectly good position," and dismissed her.

At the door of his office she hesitated. Her heart beating angrily, she forced herself to voice her request dispassionately. "Mr. Brimmer, I'd appreciate it if you'd wait until I've found another position before you fill this job. I'll make arrangements to stay long enough to train the new girl—"

"We'll see, Ms. McCallister," he cut in. "We'll see."

She resisted a strong urge to stick a finger in his eye and make sure he wouldn't "see" anything for a while.

Frittering and worrying away the rest of the day, Trish wondered darkly if she'd made the decision to transfer too quickly. Had she let emotions push her to the edge again? A brief fantasy about a wildly successful art career intervened. Heck, even a modestly successful art career. But it seemed too far from reality to give her much comfort.

In the midst of her mental writhing, a cheery co-worker sailed by her desk. "Come on, Trish. It's a quarter to five. You'll miss the van!"

She shook her head. She was in no mood for the chatty group that motorpooled. "Thanks, but go ahead without me. I've got a ride." Maybe Zach Tanner would be waiting outside to pick her up? She felt a tightness in her chest. Why hadn't he stayed last night? Was he too young to realize a woman needed reassurance after love? Or didn't he care? She'd even awakened this morning foolishly wondering if he'd come by to drive her to work.

One hour later, the taxi Trish flagged when Zach failed to show up was hopelessly stuck in Friday night rush-hour traffic.

Angrily fuming in the cab's backseat, she finally concluded that Zachary Tanner *didn't* care, that Gordon Brimmer should be drawn and quartered, and that the male sex in general were primitive, insensitive clods. "Uncaring beasts," she muttered, then noticed the cabdriver peering at her in his rearview mirror.

An aggravating twenty minutes later, the cab finally pulled into the alley behind her house.

"What do I owe you?" she asked the driver flatly.

"Forty-five dollars."

"Forty-five dollars?" she croaked. "Do I get to keep the cab?"

"Lady." He ground out the word. "My flat rate to Playa del Rey is forty-five bucks. Now, either you—"

Convinced he'd overcharged, she pulled out two twenties and a five and thrust them at him. "You taxi drivers are all alike." Leveling a deadly glare at him, she briefly considered pulling her gun and scaring the daylights out of him. "You take advantage of women" —she got out, turned and pointed at him—"drive them around, make love to them in the backseat and then toss them aside."

"What?" he sputtered incredulously. "Lady—I never made love to you anywhere—"

"No excuses. You're uncaring beasts, and you should all be shot!" As she reached in her purse for her keys, his eyes widened.

Dust churned from the cab's spinning back tires as he hit the accelerator, then barreled down the alley.

Once inside, Trish sighed heavily, plunked down on the couch and propped her feet up on the coffee table. Craning her neck to the left, she focused a sour stare at the wooden easel at the end of the couch. Zach Tanner seemed to be staring at her. The picture looked far less a masterpiece at this angle. She regretted ever having painted the darn thing, regretted even more what had happened afterward.

She frowned, suddenly angry at herself. Why are you making such a big deal out of this, McCallister? It was a physical attraction, that's all, she argued silently. Sex with a man who turned you on. Nothing more.

Would she ever learn to be casual about sex? A sigh broke inside. Casual? *Never.* Never with him.

Shaking her head, she got up, walked to the bay window and stared out at the moonless sky. "Look at you, Trish McCallister, mooning around over a twenty-six-year-old taxi driver when you have a finished painting and a man like Anton Gregory just waiting to see your work. *Anton Gregory?* Call him, dummy!"

The coffee table rattled as she marched across the living room.

Phone in hand, poised to dial, she hesitated. Why did it feel so wrong? She'd intended all along to show the painting to Gregory, hadn't she? *Yes, but shouldn't she at least tell Zach first?* Why? It was *her* picture. Posing didn't give him any rights to its disposition.

Cold logic and hot emotions took opposing sides and

battled it out for several minutes. She didn't want to deceive Zach. He'd posed night after night for no pay, his only purpose to help her. Or so he'd said. . . . How did she know what his purpose was? Maybe it was ego. Or maybe . . . ? Maybe it was a way to get into her jeans? Oooh!! That thought stung and hurt and rankled. But it explained why he'd left so abruptly afterward. He had what he wanted, the devil. The despicable devil!

Cold logic won.

A woman answered on the third ring. "Mr. Gregory's residence. May I help you?"

"This is Trish McCallister. I'm a personal friend of Mr. Gregory's. I'd like to speak with him, please."

"I'm sorry, but Mr. Gregory isn't available. He's leaving on a European holiday tomorrow, and he's asked me to screen all calls."

"Oh, but I'm sure he'll talk to me," she protested. "You see, I'm an artist and a friend of his. I have a painting I know he'll want to see before he goes."

"What's your name again, dear?" the woman asked perfunctorily.

"Trish McCallister. It's really quite urgent. Please tell him I'm waiting."

The line went silent. She'd been put on hold.

A moment later, the anonymous female voice returned. "I'm afraid he's gone out for the evening. Do you wish to leave a message?"

Trisha's heart sank. "Yes," she sighed. "Please ask him to call me back as soon as he comes in. It doesn't matter how late."

After leaving her number, she listlessly hung up the phone. Her chances of seeing Gregory before he left looked bleak at best. She briefly wondered if he was avoiding her. Had she made him angry? Offended him? Or had Zach? Questions tumbled through her mind. Suddenly it was all too confusing. *"Men,"* she grumbled. And they said women were confusing.

She slumped in the chair like a defeated boxer. Was everything destined to go wrong today? A cloud of despair settled around her. She felt tired, so tired. All she wanted was to put on her cuddly flannel nightie, go to bed and sleep.

On her weary way to the bedroom, she brushed the easel's leg and jarred the painting from its perch. "Oh, no," she cried, reflexively catching the canvas with her hands. Trembling, she placed it back on the easel and shut her eyes. He *was* beautiful, her taxi driver. What would Anton Gregory have thought of him?

Feeling shaky and close to crying, she hurried into the bedroom, pulled off her clothes and slipped into her nightie. A new best-seller waited to be read on her night table. She pulled the covers up around her, picked it up and read halfheartedly. She was barely through the first chapter when the doorbell rang.

Her heart skipped. She sprang up, a name instantly forming on her lips. *Zach,* it must be Zach. Without bothering with her robe, she ran through the house.

Her hand shook on the lock as she freed it, twisted the knob and threw the door open.

"Oh!" She stumbled backward.

Anton Gregory, tall and spare in a deep blue tuxedo, stood facing her, his eyes every bit as unholy as the first day she'd stared up at them.

6

Momentarily speechless, Trish came close to swinging the door shut in Gregory's fearsome face. *Stop it, you ninny,* she argued with herself, forcing a smile. *He's here.* This is your chance.

"Mr.—Gregory?" she faltered, wishing he would smile or otherwise alter his hawklike stare. She felt like a quivering rabbit about to be clutched in his talons.

Looking shadowy and sinister, he walked into the room.

Trish's survival instincts surged. What had that gung-ho karate instructor taught them in her women's self-defense class? In a frontal attack, go for the eyes, then when the attacker is blinded, a knee to the groin—hard! Stiffening, she waited to see what Gregory would do.

The expression on his face became oddly intense. His head tilted and twisted; his brow puckered and frowned. Suddenly Trish realized he wasn't looking at her at all.

"What's that?" he demanded, brushing past her as he walked toward the easel.

"Oh—that," she stammered, immensely relieved. "That's the painting I told your secretary about. Apparently you got my message? Is that why you've come?"

Ignoring her question, he concentrated on the painting. She watched, fascinated, as his eyes darted avidly about the canvas. A tic moved a muscle in his jaw.

"Mr. Gregory?" she hazarded finally.

He transferred his stare, and his gaze traveled her form like a flatiron, practically scorching the flowers off the flannel nightie she wore.

Oh, heavens, she worried silently. Why didn't I put on my robe? At least she had on heavy flannel and not one of those filmy nylon things she'd been saving for the right man. Folding her arms protectively over her chest, she attempted a diversion by nodding toward the easel. "The painting, Mr. Gregory? I'd like very much to know what you think."

"Hmmmm? Oh—of course, my dear." He nodded. The civility in his tone settled her uneasiness a bit.

He returned to the painting, his eyebrows knitting. He nodded once, then shook his head and stepped back to look again. After a moment, he walked to the far corner of the room, made a half turn and squinted.

A new kind of anxiety built as Trish waited.

He strode to the easel, felt the paint with his forefinger, then continued to scrutinize the painting at close range—all the while shaking his head and mumbling things that to Trish's nervous ears sounded fearfully derogatory.

By the time he turned to her, she was prepared for the worst.

"Sit down, Trish," he ordered, walking to the window. Scrupulously manicured nails tapped once, twice on the pane, and then he looked over his shoulder at her. "The painting is . . . good."

"Good?" she echoed, somehow relieved and disappointed at the same time.

After a long moment, he tapped the pane again, then turned to face her. "I must admit I'm tempted to break the rules this time."

Gulping, she clasped her hands nervously.

"I never allow myself to be obviously enthusiastic with new protégés," he continued, "even if they deserve it. Praise is often more deleterious than criticism to a neophyte." His glance flickered to the painting and back to her. With an air of studied resignation, he walked to the couch and sat. "But there's something about you—a seeming lack of ego, of artistic pretension, if you will—that encourages me. Somehow I sense you can handle the truth—even *need* to hear it—"

She waited, half crazy, while his attention was momentarily diverted to smoothing the lines of his tuxedo jacket. Finally he looked up. "The painting is more than good, actually. It's closer to . . . well, for lack of a better word, extraordinary."

She gripped her hands fiercely. "Extr—extraordinary?"

"Oh yes, my dear." He nodded and with a theatrical gesture acknowledged the easel. "There is raw, vibrant energy, and yet—" He hesitated, rose and walked to the easel. "The movement, the lines, the transitions of tone and value are at once subtle and unselfconsciously dramatic." He pursed his lips. "It is rough, to be sure, but still marvelous. Inspired—an inspired effort. And you"—he turned to her—"are to be congratulated.

"But—" He raised an eyebrow at Trish, who, too stunned to move, gaped at him. "You are also, quite irrefutably, in need of additional training. Yes—" He nodded once. "Although the implicit energy in this painting overcomes its flaws, you cannot hope to bluff your way through future work without guidance." The eyebrow arched at a precarious angle. "If you intend to be a success."

Trish got up unsteadily. "I do."

"Good." He smiled, inclining his head gallantly. "Then let me tell you what I propose." Folding his arms purposefully, he paced the room. "I'll postpone my trip a few days—yes, yes, and we'll have a private showing. As soon as possible—" His gaze lifted upward. "Tomorrow? Hmmmm? Why not? I can have all the essential people there with a few phone calls." He looked at Trish. "I'll need to see the rest of your work. The nude will be the focal point, of course, but we'll fill out the show with some of your other paintings—assuming they're reasonably good."

Her breathing shallow, she led him into the spare bedroom where he scrutinized, then set aside a watercolor, two acrylics and four oils. "These are not of the same caliber as the nude, of course, but they will do nicely," he decreed finally, sounding as surprised as she felt. Nodding as he strode from the room, he announced his intention to summon his limousine driver. "I think we'll have an excellent showing overall."

While the driver, under Gregory's officious supervision, transported and stored the unframed canvases in the limousine's interior, Trish waited, her heart doing flip-flops from all the excitement.

She hovered by the front door until Gregory returned and announced the task was finished and that he'd instructed the driver to wait.

"Let me get you something to drink," she offered.

"No," he said, looking deeply into her eyes. "If we are to have a business association, there are some things I must know about you."

"Oh?" Her stomach dipped.

He led her to the couch. She took the far end and seriously considered moving to the chair.

"First," he started, "there's the standard biographical data. We'll have a brochure printed up with your background—prior training, any early influences in the development of your style, artists you admire, personal notes, a picture if you have one—"

She grabbed notepaper and a pen from the kitchen counter and scribbled down the information as he went on at length, detailing everything he'd need.

"That should do it," he told her finally. "My secretary will call you tomorrow to let you know what time to be at the gallery. Considering the arrangements to be made, the showing will be late afternoon, I should guess, at the earliest."

Showing? she thought dazedly. Was this really happening? "Anton, are you sure about all this? I mean I've never had a showing before—"

He shook his head and laughed. "Sure? My dear, in the eminent domain of art, surety does not exist, thank God. How abominably dull! On the other hand, a little edge now and then can be very comforting." He smiled sagely. "For without it, what are we but the hapless beneficiaries of public and critical whim? Tomorrow is a gamble, but with my edge and your rather remarkable work, I'd like to think the odds are . . . propitious."

Propitious. She rolled the syllables in her head. What a lovely word.

"And now"—he smiled—"if I may venture into more personal territory."

His eyes reminded her she still had only a nightgown on. With a quick breath, she nodded. "All right."

"You may decline, of course, to answer any of my questions, but I like to know my, ah . . . protégés on more than just a business basis—"

And his models, too, she thought nervously, remembering Jacques and Avril.

"Your nude"—he indicated the easel where the painting of Zach had been—"looks familiar. Is it a recent work?" As Trish nodded, he continued. "There is an immediacy in the painting—one might almost call it raw sensuality. I could not help but wonder if he—the model—was more than just a model?" He hesitated. "Forgive me, but a lover, perhaps?"

Trish lowered her eyes. Good question, she thought

bitterly. A flash of hurt and anger made her rise and walk across the room. A lover? Did one night in the backseat of a taxi make Zach her lover? "No." She shook her head and stared at the empty easel. "Not a lover . . . just a model."

"But surely there is someone . . . or many . . . lovers? A beautiful woman—"

"Would it matter?" she cut in, uncomfortable with his probing.

"No—" He retreated. "Only in the sense that entanglements might interfere with your artistic commitment—"

"There are no such entanglements," she assured him.

"I see."

Did Gregory's voice have a slight quiver in it? She heard him rise and come up behind her.

"Anton?" she said without turning.

"Trish," he responded in a low, rustling voice. "Again I must break my rules and confess the truth. I'm deeply pleased you're to be my protégée. I find your work incredibly stimulating. We're going to be good together, my dear."

She heard him step closer and felt his breath on the back of her neck. A bony hand gripped her shoulder.

"Anton, it's late. I'm exhausted and very nervous about tomorrow."

He massaged her shoulder. "Let me help you relax—"

Feeling his body press up behind her, she shifted her shoulder, trying to casually shrug off his hand. "I—I'd prefer to be alone—"

"You have a talent that's powerful and primitive. I saw it in your painting." His voice cracked tremulously. "It excites me, Trish. You excite me. I want to explore that inner power with you—"

"Anton, no—"

His words came hot and fast. His breath burnt her

neck. "There's no need for you to be *just* a protégée, my dear. I'd like much more," he whispered harshly, his hand kneading her shoulder. "We could inspire each other—you as my talented and beautiful ina-morata."

His hand slipped down her arm and then planted itself on her breast.

"Anton—stop!" Her cry was muffled as his other hand came around and clamped over her mouth. Panic rose as she struggled to free herself. Despite his thin-ness, he was incredibly strong. There must be some civilized way to turn him off, she thought desperately. She had so much to lose!

"Trish," he cried, "your struggling excites me! Damn, how I want you—"

His hand left her breast to grope with her flannel nightgown. As he pulled it up, she reacted instinctively. Self-defense tactics asserted themselves automatically. With a guttural martial arts cry, she drove her elbow into his stomach.

"Ooooophhhh!" He released her. Eyes bulging, he doubled over.

She whirled out of the range of his grasp, and while he was still doubled up, applied a well-aimed kick to the back of his ankle, knocking his foot out from under him. With a startled grunt, the upended Anton Gregory hit the living-room floor.

He lay there a moment, groaning, obviously stunned.

Gasping for breath, Trish watched, equally stunned. What had she done? There was her art career on the floor.

He stopped groaning long enough to open his eyes and look at her warily. "No—no more," he moaned as she bent to try to help. Waving away her hand, he rolled to his stomach and began to push himself to his knees.

Trish's eyes widened in horror. He was coming up under the extended edge of her glass coffee table. Too late to stop him, she saw his head collide with the thick glass ledge. The resounding thwack vibrated the entire table. With a muffled grunt, he revisited the floor.

"Oh, no," Trish cried. Pulling him over onto his back, she gasped. His eyes rolled in their sockets and then fluttered shut. "He's unconscious," she wailed, "or *dead!*" Summoning enough presence of mind to take his pulse, she discovered with relief that he was only unconscious.

She quickly pulled off the tuxedo's black silk tie, undid the shirt's high collar, propped his head on a sofa pillow and fanned him with a copy of *New Woman* magazine. "Anton, please, *please* wake up," she pleaded. Dear God, she didn't want to call the paramedics. Tomorrow's headlines would scream: Eminent Artist Viciously Assaulted by Woman in Flannel Nightgown.

What would bring him to? She ran to the kitchen and dampened a dishrag. After several minutes of bathing his pale face, she was dismayed to find he still didn't respond.

Sitting back on her haunches, she looked at the peacefully unresponsive form and grimaced in frustration. Stubborn man, she thought rather hysterically. If he hadn't molested her, this never would have happened. And now, even though it was *his* fault, he was going to abuse her further by refusing to wake up.

In the movies she'd seen them slap people to consciousness. The idea seemed too good to be true. No, she thought suddenly. *Cold water.* They always doused unconscious people with cold water. She stood, vacillating, then rushed to the kitchen. It was an infinitely better idea than calling the paramedics.

Returning from the kitchen with a full pitcher, she positioned herself over his head. Do it, Trish, she ordered. To hell with his blue satin tuxedo. Just as she tipped the pitcher, his eyes blinked open. Unable to react fast enough to avert the cold water's momentum, she saw him look up groggily and open his mouth to protest.

She would never know what he'd planned to say. The waterfall garbled his words into oblivion.

Sputtering, gasping, he pushed himself to a sitting position, then moaned and crumpled back to his elbows. "Do you intend to kill me?" he wailed, aghast, his features pinched in pain.

"No!" she cried. "No—of course not." She dropped penitently to her knees. "Oh God, I'm so sorry. I mean I had to sort of . . . hit you in the stomach and then . . . trip you, but I didn't knock you out. *Really.* You hit your head on the coffee table when you tried to get up."

He groaned miserably, rubbed his head and eyed her suspiciously. "That wasn't you who just tried to drown me?"

"Well, yes, that was me," she admitted, "but I had to. You wouldn't come to." Smiling weakly, hopefully, she brushed water from the wilted collar of his tuxedo. "Anyway, it worked."

As he shifted away and struggled to sit up, she shrewdly refrained from offering her assistance. He fretted and fussed, discovering new wounds like an injured child.

Hoping he'd begun to compose himself, she asked finally, "Are you okay?"

He stopped nursing the bump on his head and looked at her incredulously. "You mean other than the concussion, the water in my lungs, and the bruised muscles in my stomach?"

"Oh, Anton, I'm sorry. Truly, truly I am, but you came up behind me—"

"That I did." He grimaced. "God help me if I ever make that mistake again."

"Anton," she pleaded, "let me help you up. Wouldn't you be more comfortable on the couch?" She jumped up and started for the kitchen. "I'll get an ice pack for your head."

"No!" he cried, looking at her as though she were a certifiable lunatic. "An ice pack in your hands could be deadly. My body may be broken, but my sanity is still intact." He staggered to his feet. "There are laws to dispense with people who are a danger to themselves or others. You"—he looked over at her, one eye squeezed shut in pain—"qualify on both counts."

There it is, Trish, she sighed morosely, what'd you expect? He'll never forgive you. The career's bilge water. And he intends to sic the police on you into the bargain.

From arm's length distance, she offered him a box of tissues and watched as he worked valiantly to make himself presentable again.

With each passing moment she grew more indignant. Why was she solely to blame? Who, after all, had started this fiasco? "I'll tell your driver to come and help you to the car," she asserted, wanting more than anything to have this fastidious lecher out of her house. Halting at the door, she turned back defiantly, sure she knew the answer but determined to ask the question anyway. "What about the paintings? Shall I tell your driver to bring them back in the house?"

Smoothing back his graying hair, he looked perplexed. "Whatever for? Have you changed your mind about the showing?"

Hope flickered. "Me? Of course not, but after what just happened—"

He shrugged graciously, a damp smile flickering on his lips. "I think it might be best all around if we forgot what just happened."

"Me too," she blurted.

"I don't want to lose a potentially gifted artist because of a . . . let's call it a rather painful misunderstanding."

"And I certainly don't want to lose a mentor."

In the awkward moment that followed, a thought surfaced—one that had been forming ever since he'd decided to take her work. "Anton," she said slowly, "I know this is incredibly bad timing and probably premature of me, but I'd rather you didn't . . . well, that you didn't sell the painting—the nude, I mean—without talking to me first. Okay?" She smiled weakly.

He looked confused. She had the feeling he wanted to argue but couldn't summon the strength. "Very well," he sighed. Hobbling around to her door, he muttered, "Never mind calling the driver. I can make it."

"Are you sure? Let me help you," she offered impulsively, then stepped back at the look on his face. "Sorry."

She followed him, maintaining a safe distance as he made his way out. To her surprise, he stopped on the porch, turned stiffly and called her to him. As she approached he pressed a brief, avuncular kiss to her forehead. "If one of us must always be on the floor when we meet," he declared dryly, "I prefer it be you." Punctuating his pained smile with a brave wink, he turned and stumbled down the porch steps and around the side of the house. Leaning against the door frame, she smiled fondly. A man with a sense of humor can't be all bad, she decided generously.

Then she turned to go inside, wishing she knew where to find Zach so she could tell him what had happened and was about to happen.

Even with a couple hundred pairs of skeptical eyes fastened on her, Trish fought and somehow managed to continue breathing. The intimate, private showing had inexplicably mushroomed, Anton explained in whispers as Trish perched on a director's chair on the small, raised platform she shared with Zach's painting. "It's all right," she whispered back gamely, intuiting that he was nearly as nervous as she was. "So long as *you* do the talking." She wisely refrained from telling him she intended to get through it all by nodding and waving and pretending she was a Rose Bowl queen. The fantasy she'd indulged in since childhood had seen her through other moments of extreme fear—although none so extreme as this.

As Anton went off to double-check the arrangements, she watched anxiously as the elite and the curious filed into the gallery. Fifteen minutes later, he ordered the doors closed and asked for the crowd's attention.

Despite the prominent bandage on the back of his head, Anton was indefatigably elegant and eloquent as he introduced her.

". . . and I predict that this young woman is about to set the art world on its . . . ear," he finished, with a sidelong glance at Trish. "But judge for yourselves, ladies and gentlemen. You see her work here before you. It awaits your consideration." Encouraging them to partake of the food and drink, he took Trish's arm and led her around to meet wealthy patrons of the arts, prominent local artists and critics and the insatiably curious press corps.

Desperately awed, Trish smiled and nodded while Anton fielded questions.

Two hours later, the crowd began to disperse. Thoroughly exhausted, Trish had discovered the secret of successful royalty—a double-jointed neck. Would her head ever stop bobbing? Would she still be nodding and smiling like a car-dashboard ornament days later?

A new wave of excitement restored her as a critic came up to commend her on the "dormant strength" in her work. As Anton spirited him away, she surveyed the scene dazedly. All this? For her? Was it possible? She felt dizzy, giddy. Much too light and airy to be connected to the ground. Watch it, Trish, she warned. No accidents today, *please*.

From somewhere in the gallery, a silver glint diverted her attention. Stiffening, she scanned the room, sure she'd seen the flash of silver eyes. Was it *him*? Was he here?

Over the heads of the departing crowd, she saw him. He stood poised against the far wall of the gallery, his gaze hard as stainless steel.

Zach, she breathed silently.

Unmoving, he assaulted her with a lethal stare, then turned away and pushed through the throng toward the door.

Stunned by his presence and his obvious fury, she watched him leave, unable to call, to follow. As he disappeared through the door, she broke loose and rushed after him, jostling the startled patrons. But he was gone.

As she returned to the gallery, a strange, pervasive listlessness crept through her. Had she really seen him? Had he been there at all? She shivered and looked around the emptying room. The people, the paintings, even the building seemed flattened and one-dimensional. Were her eyes playing tricks? Was any of this real?

Feeling a disturbing inner stillness, she turned to see Anton extending polite thanks and good-byes at the doorway. He seemed lifeless and brittle—a cardboard cutout with movable arms and legs. They all were! A room full of billboard figures. Nothing was real? No one was real? Numbness seeped through her senses. Energy drained from her limbs.

She found a chair, sat and shut her eyes. Was exhaustion fouling her senses? Or was she slipping into the twilight zone? Suddenly it all seemed completely absurd, and she heard herself laughing—a tiny, hysterical laugh.

Anton's voice came to her as though from far away. "Trish? What's wrong? Are you ill?"

"I don't know." Overwhelmed with fatigue, she tried to tell him, but all she could say was "I don't know. . . ."

She awoke groggily, stretched, then sat up with a start. The unfamiliar surroundings alerted her thought processes. A bedside lamp illumined the formal, almost regal bedroom. Was that Anton? Yes, asleep in a chair beside a smoldering fireplace. It took a moment before she remembered.

A doctor, one of the guests at the showing, had diagnosed her as suffering from exhaustion and nerves.

He'd given her a sedative and had written out a prescription for more, with instructions to get plenty of rest and quiet. Anton, in a fit of paternal concern, had taken her to fill the prescription and then had insisted on bringing her here, to his Malibu beach house. She'd apparently gone into a near coma as soon as she had a mattress beneath her.

A small, ornate table clock said four thirty-five. She looked lazily out windows curtained in satin brocade. It was dark out there. Unless she'd slept twenty-four hours straight, it must be morning, *early* morning.

Lying back down, she pulled the downy comforter up around her and remembered: the simply gorgeous, deeply satisfying gallery opening. She snuggled rapturously. It hadn't been a dream, not for a moment. It was all tangible and material and real. And so was Zach, she thought, saddening.

She shifted onto her side, feeling silken sheets caress her arms as she moved. With an involuntary shiver, she remembered the misted windows of Zach's taxi, the sensuous whispers, the bodies driven with need of each other.

"Are you awake?" Anton's voice came from across the room.

"Umm-hmm." Sitting up, she pulled the sheet up for cover, then realized she still had her dress on.

He walked over and sat on the edge of the bed. "Feeling better?"

She nodded and shrugged. "A little too much excitement, I guess." Some of us weren't cut out to be Rose Bowl queens, she thought ironically.

He smiled in agreement.

"Anton," she asked, her fingers crossed. "How did the showing go? Really. Tell me the truth."

He straightened his crumpled smoking jacket. "The doctor said you were to have quiet—no excitement."

Her eyes beseeched him.

"Trish," he insisted, "I just don't know yet. An initial

response, even if favorable, doesn't always mean anything in terms of sales. Time will tell if they intend to buy what they've praised, or if it was just idle talk."

"But there was praise?" she asked. "Even from the critics?"

Nodding, he stood. "With a few exceptions among the stuffier of the breed. And unless it was lip service or temporary deference to me, you'll have very creditable reviews."

Her ego soared like a space-bound rocket. Very creditable? She mentally pooh-poohed Anton's conservatism. The man was a model of restraint. *They loved her!* They would clamor to buy paintings by Patricia McCallister! She bounded out of bed and hugged him, then began to hunt for her shoes. "Anton, please take me home."

"No," he protested. "You're to rest—"

"I'll rest at home," she insisted. She had to be alone where she could savor and rerun every moment over and over. *She was an artist. Her work had been praised.*

Anton helped Trish from the sleek green Ferrari and walked her around to her door. "I'll say good-bye here," he said, hesitating on the porch.

"I'd invite you in," she explained, "but I really need to be alone."

He raised a conciliatory hand, then pointed to the bandage on his head. "Just as well. I don't have a crash helmet handy—"

With a delighted laugh, she kissed him. "I have so much to thank you for. I don't know how to begin."

"Next time I come up behind you," he advised, an evil glint in his eye, "don't struggle quite so hard."

"Next time *don't* come up behind me," she tossed back, discouraging the salacious smile. "Will you call me as soon as you hear anything?"

Regaining his typical equanimity, he assured her he would and left.

In anticipation of blessed solitude, she inserted her key in the dead-bolt lock and turned it. Her stomach knotted as she realized the door was unlocked. Heart pounding, she gave it a light push and watched it swing open. Slowly, carefully, she looked about, then stepped inside.

In the corner, next to the empty easel, Zach waited. Legs braced wide, arms crossed, he looked like the eye of a hurricane as an aura of blue-white anger enveloped him.

7

Zach tensed, every muscle straining at the sound of steps on the front porch. A vein pulsed in his forehead. The cumulative rage that had corroded his insides for the past forty-eight hours boiled up fresh and hot.

He watched their silhouettes against the window-pane. Gregory's hovering stick figure. The upward incline of her chin as their lips touched like lovers. *Lovers.* "Bastard," he hissed, fists clenching painfully. And *her.* How could she do it? Had her body even cooled from their passion before she'd offered herself to Gregory? Now he knew what that damn painting was all about—a way to get to Gregory.

Anger surged and clotted in his throat. A spasm twisted his heart. After observing them together for the past two days, he'd discovered a new kind of pain—it ripped at him like a stiletto, it wouldn't let him forget, and now, watching them together, it wouldn't let him forgive.

Gregory's muffled insinuations carried through the glass. A barely tempered fury coiled inside Zach like a spring. His hands stretched rigid, then clenched again, aching to snap his rival's skinny frame in two.

A warning flashed inside his head. He was a ticking bomb that had only to see her walk through that door to detonate.

"Get out of here now, Tanner," he muttered, "before someone gets hurt." Wheeling around, he started for the back door. As he reached the easel, the front door clicked. He whirled around. The door swung open. She hesitated, looked about with wary eyes and stepped inside.

His eyes scored her body. She was messy and unkempt—a woman tousled from another man's bed. His mind tortured him with explicit snapshots of her, wantonly stretched beneath Gregory. A lethal rage burned through him. He took a step toward her before a tenuous saving instinct held him back. Or was it the fear in those huge brown eyes that stopped him?

Her mouth opened, then quivered with unuttered words. A soft, plummy mouth. His stomach tugged. Unbelievable—he wanted to kiss her. Another snapshot froze his desire. Were those lips still warm from Gregory's? How had she kissed him? And where? Had she moaned and cried and begged *him* for more? Anger surged. His arm went rigid. A fist formed. Cords distended from his neck like cables.

"Zach? Where have you been?" she asked tremulously.

Oh God, he wanted to hold her . . . but he couldn't —he hated her. It was his only defense against her.

She started toward him, and he went rigid. *"No!"* The harsh command stopped her. Snap out of it, man, he ordered. Stop this insanity. You came here to get answers. Do it. *Or get out before you hurt her.*

"Zach, why didn't you come back?" Her words pelted him like hailstones. Her questioning innocence choked him. "So many things have happened," she rushed on. "I wanted to tell you, but I didn't know how to reach you—"

"I did come back," he forced out.

She frowned. "What? When?"

His voice cut, a serrated knife blade. "Two nights ago. You were out there on the porch with Anton Gregory—in a nightgown. You kissed him—"

"Oh! No—" she cut in, gasping. "It wasn't like that. He kissed me on the forehead. And the nightgown—I had that on when he arrived. I mean—" The words dropped off helplessly.

Her hesitation confirmed his suspicions. It's true. She slept with Gregory. The night after being with me, she slept with him. A fierce pain socked the breath out of him. "Where were you last night?" he demanded. The furious coil tightened as he waited to hear her lie to his face.

Small fires kindled in her eyes, burning away the fear. "I was at Anton's," she blurted defiantly, "but it's not what you think. Dammit, Zach, *listen to me!* Let me tell you what's happened."

Listen to her? No, no . . . No—he couldn't listen to her. She'd been with him. He'd seen them together—two nights before, and then at the showing, and last night—all night at Gregory's beach house. No—he wouldn't listen to her. She would lie—or even worse, tell him the truth. And he couldn't handle either!

"I did not sleep with Anton," she announced flatly. Her eyes dared him to question her.

"Don't lie," he whispered. "Don't lie to me!"

She walked to him, looked straight into his eyes and repeated, "I didn't sleep with Anton."

He caught the scent of expensive men's cologne. It seared his nostrils. "You're lying," he spat. "You smell of him."

"What?" she backed up, her eyes desperate. "But how—? Wait—I know, I know. It was nothing, I hugged him, that's all—" She took a step back. "Zach! Please stop looking at me that way—" With a ragged gasp, she turned away.

He caught her arm and spun her back, his fingers notching her skin with scarlet marks. An icy, heartless sound came from somewhere inside him. "How does he do it, Mac? Rough?" His fingers tightened, biting into her soft skin like wire.

"Why didn't you tell me you wanted it that way? I could have satisfied those baser drives. Hell, I still can." With a vicious jerk he pulled her to him. Soft breasts pillowed against his chest as he gripped the back of her neck and forced her mouth to meet his. He kissed her hard. "Is this how you like it?" he snarled against her lips.

"Stop it!" she hissed, pushing against him with all her strength.

"What?" He backed away, a cruel smirk on his face. "Not in the mood? Or maybe you think I can't meet your price? You got what you wanted from the poor dumb taxi driver, so you're done with him—is that it?"

"You bastard!" she cried as he wrenched her back against him. "Let go of me!"

He froze as a shockwave went through him. What was he doing?

Releasing her, he looked down at his hands as though they belonged to someone else. As she averted her face, he hesitantly reached out and touched a large, slow-rolling tear.

Get out of here, a voice inside him warned. You're borderline crazy, Tanner. She's got a grip on your insides—those frail fingers will turn and twist your vitals until you go insane. Didn't I tell you, the voice grated. Didn't I tell you to stay clear of her? You're going to blow it, man. You're out of control.

He heard her take a breath.

His heart hurt with every beat. Turning, he strode toward the door.

"Zach—?" Her voice followed him like a child's cry. Plaintive, it clung to him like wispy fabric. Keep going, he ordered fiercely.

"Wait—" she entreated as he pushed open the door.

"Don't go—!" The cry followed him as he broke and ran to his car.

A phone rang somewhere in the distance. Far, far away. Too far away to answer. Seeking to blot out the noise, she pulled the covers over her head. But it didn't go away. It inched closer, louder, each shrill more insistent, and finally forced her to waking consciousness.

Her hand reached out, found the receiver and pulled it under the covers.

"Trish? Are you there?"

". . . ummmm."

"What is it? What's wrong?"

Despite her groggy state, she recognized Anton's voice.

"Nothing," she mumbled. "I took some of those sedatives the doctor gave me."

"Some? How many?" There was fear in his voice.

"Only two," she sleepily reassured him.

"Well, at least I don't have to worry about my news overstimulating you."

"News? What is it?" She pulled the covers off her head.

"I've got the evening papers here." She heard the rustle of papers at his end and looked at her bedside clock. It was 6:00 P.M. She'd slept all day. Sometime after Zach left, she didn't know when, she'd stumbled into bed and tried to extinguish her inner turmoil with sleep. But his anguished violence haunted her. She was unable even to shut her eyes. In desperation, she had resorted to the sedatives.

". . . mixed reviews. . . ." Anton's words penetrated.

"What?"

"A couple of them predict you'll be a new artistic trendsetter. One says your work is 'rife with subtle erotic incantations.' Another says it raised the hair on her arms—that's a quote. Unfortunately, one party pooper advises you to switch to doing covers for romantic novels, and another found it too blatantly, obviously sexual in tone—"

"My God, Anton—" she said, sitting up. "What does it all mean? Was I good or bad?"

"According to the critics, it's a toss-up, but they're only half the story—the lesser half. Get a grip on something, Trish—"

"What? Why?"

"I've already had a half-dozen calls to buy your nude, and every time I politely decline they boost their bids."

"They want to buy my painting? Who? How much?"

"Women, mostly. Wealthy, widowed and probably wildly lonely women. And men, too. One of the art critics even made an offer on your still life. Ridiculously low. Of course I turned him down."

"Turned him down? Anton, I'd be lucky to *give* that still life away."

"Not anymore, dear. Your nude is hot and so are you. I'm personally commissioning you, as of this moment, to do five more paintings—just for starters. And have your lawyer contact mine first thing in the morning to draw up an agreement. Other than my standard percentages, my only stipulation will be that you show exclusively at my galleries for the next—say, two years? And of course, during that time period, I'll defray the cost of showings and publicity, and guarantee the right audience—"

"Anton, you're going too fast. I don't have a lawyer—"

"Oh?" He paused as if she were the first person he'd ever encountered who didn't have a lawyer on retainer. "Well . . . you're welcome to use mine. Why don't I arrange a meeting? If you feel comfortable, we'll have him draw up the agreement. If not, you can have whatever time you need to find your own representation. Does that sound fair?"

"Yes," she said feebly. "More than fair." Her mind went to Zach. Oh, the tricks of fate, she thought miserably. Why now? In her state of mind, she'd be lucky to be able to pick up a brush, much less complete a painting. Why were they clamoring for her work now . . . ?

Anton's voice, insistently providing further details, hammered through her insecurities.

Trish checked her watch as the Yellow cab pulled into the alley. Seven-fifteen. Even if the traffic was still heavy, she'd easily make her meeting with Gordon Brimmer by 9:00 A.M. She wasn't taking any chances on offending "Numero Uno."

Anton had insisted over the phone last night that she quit her job. She'd decided privately, and much less recklessly, to take a leave of absence. Such an arrangement would require Brimmer's and the personnel department's approval. The latter was no problem. The former—well, she'd soon know.

"The Great Western Bank Building on Wilshire and Western," she informed the cabbie, noticing with subdued amusement that it was the same man she'd tongue-lashed the previous Friday night. He acted as though he didn't recognize her. Just as well, she thought gratefully. She wanted a quiet ride to plan her pitch to Brimmer.

The ride passed slowly, uneventfully. Among her other mental deliberations, Trish realized she would have to buy a car if she was to work at Gregory's studio. She couldn't afford taxi drivers who charged, and there would be no car pool to Malibu and back. She still had the insurance payoff from her Celica stashed away in a savings account—that should be enough for something secondhand.

She stared blankly out the side window, her mind full of halfhearted plans. As the taxi pulled up and stopped at an intersection, she noticed the old green Plymouth lumbering by in the cross traffic.

"My God!" she blurted, straightening. "Take a left! Follow that cab!"

"Huh?" The driver looked in the rearview mirror. His eyes narrowed. "Hey—were you in this cab last week?"

"No," she lied. The light turned green. "Go left," she insisted, craning her neck to keep Zach's cab in view. "Go left!"

"I can't, lady. I'm in the wrong lane—"

"You *have* to. If I lose him now, I may never find him again! Turn, dammit!"

"No way, lady." He glared at her in the mirror and shook his head. "I ain't gettin' involved in no chase scene—"

The cars behind them were beginning to honk. Trish saw the right turn signal blink on Zach's taxi. He was about to make a turn. She would lose him. *She would never see him again.* Her mind grasped at options. There was no time! Fumbling through her purse, she found the gun and pressed it behind the driver's ear. "This is a weapon in my hand," she blurted nervously. What was the penalty for kidnapping a taxi? "Take a left here and follow that green Plymouth."

She nearly toppled over as the driver, horn blaring, wrenched left and forced his way through an intersection filled with moving human and vehicular targets.

"There! See—he's turning. Follow him," Trish ordered, waving the gun.

The taxi careened right, clipped the curve, nearly sideswiped a delivery truck, and shot after the Plymouth.

Trish gulped and hung on to the seat back. Just her luck to get a driver who thought he was Evel Knievel. Or maybe the gun was making him nervous? "Calm down," she soothed him.

"Calm down?" he croaked. "You want calm? You drive and I'll hold the gun." He swerved from lane to lane like a speed-drunk race-car driver.

She gripped the seat back and braced herself as he veered right to follow Zach up a freeway on-ramp. "If you won't calm down, at least *slow down,*" she yelped. "We're going to get arrested!"

"Ask me if I care," the cabbie muttered.

Nearly airborne, they soared onto the freeway. The cab's steel-belted radials barely touched asphalt. The gas pedal never left the floor. The crazed cabbie burned up the 405 freeway as if it were a NASCAR drag strip. Before she'd caught her breath, he'd veered into the lane behind Zach and was crowding the Plymouth close enough to trim its tailpipe.

She was riding with a maniac! Trish looked out the windows frantically for flashing red lights. The blinking eyes of adjacent motorists peered back at her.

The cabbie thumped his horn repeatedly. "Stop it," Trish snapped, and then suddenly realized the tricky devil was doing this on purpose. Ah ha! she crowed, he *wants* the police to spot us! The silly fool thinks they'll save him from getting shot. "I insist you stop that *immediately.*"

The words had barely left her mouth before he swerved right and followed Zach down a winding exit ramp. Trish lurched forward and nearly jackknifed into the front seat as his foot slammed the brakes and laid rubber for a stretch of fifty feet. They waffled to a screeching halt and barely avoided climbing the stopped Plymouth's trunk. Standing so close their bumpers kissed, the two taxis waited at the exit's red light.

"Oh, no," Trish groaned. Eyes wide, she saw Zach turn and glare through his rear window. She ducked down, only her eyes peeking over the back of the seat. For a tense moment, she thought he might get out and come back to rearrange her driver's face.

This is getting out of hand, she reasoned. Her taxi

driver simply *had* to settle down. Much as she hated armed coercion, she had no choice. The light turned green. "Now, calm down," she warned quietly, cocking the gun, "and keep your hands off that horn, or your brains will be all over the windshield."

He did as he was told.

Ten minutes later, they pulled up in front of an old apartment building in Venice. Trish ducked down and watched Zach get out, run up the steps and disappear through a weather-beaten door.

"How much do I owe you?" she asked, returning the gun to her bag.

"Don't shoot," the cabbie gurgled.

She took out a twenty and then added a five for good measure and dropped it on the front seat. "Don't bother waiting," she said, getting out.

Stepping back quickly, she watched him burn rubber down the street. The taxi's back door flapped open. She shook her head and sighed. That man's an accident begging to happen.

Focusing her thoughts on the task ahead, she started down the sidewalk toward the apartment house. One way or another, Zach Tanner was going to hear her side of the story. Her heart tap-danced nervously.

A rusty mailbox in the apartment's entrance hallway told her he was in apartment 2E.

Taking the stairway, she found his door and knocked. When no one answered, she tried the knob and then pushed open the unlocked door. The shower was running. Good—that would give her a moment to calm down. She entered and looked around the living room. So this was home? Who was his decorator? Conan the Barbarian? The place looked like a train wreck. Unable to stop herself, she knelt down to pick up some dropped clothes.

As the shower turned off, she jerked to her feet.

A moment later, Zach strode into the room and stopped short.

She dropped his clothes.

Clad only in jeans, he clenched his face in a Clint Eastwood frown. "What are you doing here?"

"I'm—I'm—" Suddenly she couldn't even remember. This is a mistake, she moaned silently. It's happening again. I can't think straight. "Nothing—I was just leaving."

"Freeze," he commanded as she reached the door.

She looked over her shoulder and saw him coming after her. "You freeze," she shrilled, pulling out the gun.

"Whoa—" He halted, hands up. "Haven't we done this before? What am I supposed to do now, drop my jeans?" His fingers went to the waistband snap.

She brandished her weapon. "Don't try it, Mr. Fastpants, if you want to live to put 'em back on. Just sit over there on the couch *and listen.*"

She reiterated minute by minute what had happened since he'd left her that night after their encounter in the taxi. When he stubbornly clung to his skepticism, she blasted him with the truth and wore him down with hairpin turns of logic. "If I were planning a rendezvous with Anton, would I be wearing a flannel nightgown?" she argued.

"All right," he conceded reluctantly, "so maybe you didn't sleep with him that time, but the next night you were with him until dawn."

"I was sick," she insisted, "from nerves, from worry, and mostly from seeing you glaring at me from the back of the gallery and then tearing out of there without a word." She took the gun in her left hand and sat down to fumble through her bag. "Here." She pulled out a small prescription vial and tossed it to Zach. "I nearly passed out from nervous exhaustion. A doctor at the showing prescribed these for me. Anton took me to his place to see that I got some rest. Nothing, I repeat, *nothing happened.* Regardless of what you may think of the man, he does not take advantage of sickly women. And if you still don't believe I was too sick for a wild fling, call the doctor's office."

Zach studied the prescription, then looked up. "You really didn't sleep with him?"

She shook her head.

With the cunning of a Green Beret, he rushed her, knocked the gun from her hand and pulled her into his arms. All before she could squeak out a protest.

"You wild, crazy female," he growled. "You know you're driving me insane, don't you?"

"It's mutual," she murmured, looking up at him. His eyes were crystals of smoky blue quartz. His jaw tensed and his lips parted expectantly, hungrily.

Trish felt a spiraling helplessness overtake her. Even if she had wanted to stop him, she couldn't. She'd never been able to, never would be able to. . . .

With a muffled cry, she took his fierce kiss, and his strong embrace stirred her to sharp, trembly shivers. How good, how incredibly good he was.

He gave a throaty sound, his hand contracting in her hair. Breaking the kiss, he held her, pressing her cheek against his chest. "What are we doing to each other, you and I?"

"I don't know," she whispered back, "but sometimes it scares me."

"Me, too." He laughed softly, pressing his lips against her hair. "You scare the hell out of me." He held her close, breathing softly, audibly. After a moment his hands gripped her forearms and held her back. "Why did you give him the painting—? Damn, I wish you hadn't."

She looked away, unaware of his clouding eyes. "Zach . . . as long as I'm being completely honest, I have to admit I intended to all along, but I didn't know how to tell you. You have this crazy idea that Anton is some nefarious rogue just waiting to catch me off guard." She paused, looked up and saw the storm warnings. "Well—even if he is, I can handle him—" Should she tell him how she'd handled him once already? Zach's eyes flashed like flares. Was he about to become unreasonable again?

"You're a talented artist, Mac. You don't need him."

"No, you're wrong. I do need him." How did she make him see there was a real world out there? That it was competitive and tough, often cutthroat. "Zach," she scolded softly. "You're being naïve. Talent is no guarantee of anything. Even if I could make it without Anton's contacts and support, it would take me *years.*"

"So it takes years, so what?"

"Oh, Zach, I'm not as young as you are—" She broke off, remembering he didn't know her age. "It's just that I've waited so long already. Why should I wait any longer when I don't have to—?"

"Don't get involved with him, Mac." It was a terse, uninflected statement.

"It's too late. I already am. He's commissioned me to do five more paintings."

His face colored angrily. "Turn him down. You can still say no."

"I don't *want* to say no. Why should I?"

He gripped her arms. "Because I'm asking, Mac. Because it will be better for everyone concerned, believe me."

"What kind of a reason is that?" Oh, it was so simple for him. "Zach, do you realize what you're doing? You're forcing me to choose between you and Anton. Why? It doesn't have to be this way." She rushed on, desperate. "My relationship with him will be *business.* It won't interfere with us, I promise." She looked up at him. "Don't do this, Zach."

He refused to meet her eyes. "I have to."

"Why?" she repeated in utter frustration. "I don't understand."

"You're the one who preaches about not judging another's necessity," he said quietly, "but now you're judging mine."

"No," she argued, "not judging—questioning. What you're asking is impossible. Why would you put such a price on our relationship?"

His jaw tightened stubbornly. "I've given you the

bottom line. Right now I can't do any more than that. Can't you just go along with me?"

"And give up the opportunity of a lifetime? Just because you think Anton's a lecher? Zach, that's ridiculous. Is there something more? For heaven's sake, tell me."

He turned away.

"Zach . . . ?" Words jumbled in her throat. She swallowed. "You're pushing me away."

"Nobody's pushing," he denied harshly. "You know the bottom line. It's your choice."

"My choice?" she whispered, horrified. "You're asking me to sacrifice my art career to soothe your male ego? How can I make a choice like that?"

He turned back, pain flickering in his eyes. "You just did," he said quietly.

Trish raced down the steps of his apartment building and out onto the street. Her chest burning with every breath, she hurried aboard the waiting westbound bus. She dropped the right change into the slot and found an empty seat. Somehow she must not cry. Not here in front of a busload of curious eyes, not even when she got home, not ever. Setting her jaw resolutely, she succeeded in holding back the tidal surge of tears. Only the tiniest quiver moved her chin. Good girl, she thought, gripping her tote bag feverishly, good girl.

A tall blond man boarded at the next stop. Was it Zach? Had he come after her? Trish waited, afraid to look, unable to breathe. No, it's not him, she realized as the man turned and took a seat. *Not him.* A sharp aching bit at her jaw. A tender, merciless stinging assailed temples and eyelids. Her face constricted with denied pain. Years of grief welled up as this fresh wound broke the tough scar tissue around her heart. You'll be all right, Trisha, she sang silently, repeatedly, chin trembling. A brokenhearted child's dirge. A tear escaped her eyes. No, no! Fragile defenses quaked. No, she cried, pinching the flesh of her thumb savagely. She would not cry. Pain shot through her hand. pain she could control. . . . .

By the time she reached home, he was part of her past. Stored away like old clothes. She would not mourn Zachary Tanner. She would not allow herself to cry. Her past was a reservoir of tears—enough for a lifetime.

A dark ache pressed her heart. She wondered if it would ever go away.

Her watch said twelve noon. She was three hours late for her meeting with Gordon Brimmer.

8

Trish—you simply must snap out of this funk you're in." Lifting the tailored pants-cuff of his black alpaca suit, Anton exposed a polished wing tip. He raised his foot and shook it free of beach sand, then repeated the impatient gesture with the other shoe.

Slumped on her portable stool, Trish stared out at the foggy beach scene. She picked up her palette, selected some paint tubes and began listlessly squeezing colors onto the board. Anton was right. She'd been staring out at slate blue breakers, lavender mistiness and swooping seagulls every morning for several days without painting a stroke. The day after her breakup with Zach two weeks before, she'd sat in her dimly lit spare room and painted mournful figures shrouded in shadowy despair. "Good grief, Trish—" Anton's eyebrow had arched in horror. "What's that supposed to be? A Tibetan funeral?" He'd clucked twice. "No, no, no, *mon chou*—this won't do at all. Your public wants life, energy, sensuality. . . ."

A rowdy seagull brought Trish back to the present. It soared overhead and decorated her palette with a splotch of white. Without thinking, she mixed in some cerulean blue, turned to her blank canvas and began to paint in the background sky.

Anton watched in dismay. "Trish? For God's sake, I'm worried about you." He knelt down, took the brush from her hand and looked her straight in the eye. "What's wrong?"

"I don't know," she lied. "I guess I'm just in a slump. Painter's block, or something."

"Are you still upset about losing your job?"

"No," she lied again. By the time she'd arrived at Grover Chemicals four hours late on that fateful day of car chases and lovers' quarrels, Brimmer had already set the corporate wheels in motion to fill her position. He hired a new administrative assistant two days later. Even George Lawson's promise that she would be first in line for the next position to open up, and Anton's promise to pay her a substantial advance on the paintings he'd commissioned, did not console her. She was possessed by a gritty fear that everything she really cared about was to be plucked from her by greedy cosmic fingers. "Don't worry," she said tonelessly, reclaiming her brush. "I'm all right."

"Don't tell me not to worry," Anton scolded, snatching back the brush. "I'm making glib promises and holding potential buyers at bay; I've postponed my European trip indefinitely, and I'm damn well going to worry until you snap out of this.

"I hope you haven't forgotten we have a binding agreement. You are to produce five paintings of the same caliber as your untitled nude—"

"I haven't forgotten anything," she defended herself. "But our agreement doesn't require that I produce them at the snap of your fingers. Anton—for heaven's sake," she pleaded, "stop rushing me. You're only making things worse."

He handed back the paintbrush, a thoughtful expression on his face. Trish could see an idea was in progress. "You're absolutely right." He nodded. "I have been pushing you. Damned insensitive of me. What you need right now is a complete change of pace."

"Change of pace?" Why didn't she like the sound of that?

"Ummmmm." He nodded in rapt thought. "And I have just the ticket. I've been planning a cruise for sometime next month—down the California coast to Cabo San Lucas. But why wait? We'll go immediately—"

"We?"

"We'll set a leisurely pace—take a week, two, whatever—"

"We?" she repeated. "You and me?"

"Yes," he said absently. "You and me and thirty or so of my dearest friends." He turned to look at her. "But no painting, do you hear me, Trish? You're to replenish your artistic reserves."

She had to admit that a cruise to Cabo San Lucas sounded lovely, unless . . . "Anton, if you have any notion of a shipboard romance—"

"My dear," he cut in, "my only notions at the moment are your renewed ability to paint and *our* subsequent economic gain."

Somehow she didn't find that at all difficult to believe. Lately, Anton had shown far more concern for the money her work might bring in than for any real talent she might harbor. Even his early insistence that she have more training had been forgotten in the clamor for her "raw, naturalistic style."

"We'll have separate sleeping quarters? No funny stuff?"

He laughed lightly. "You may have a stateroom on the opposite end of the ship if you wish. And as for funny stuff"—he patted the back of his head—"I'm not anxious for any more brain damage."

"All right," she agreed quickly. If she gave herself time to think, she'd find a million reasons not to go. And she did need to get away. Her cottage and even the ocean beach were still painful reminders. Every time she saw a taxi she felt an overwhelming urge to cry. In two weeks, there'd been no word from Zach, no sign of him, nothing. In spite of her vow not to mourn, the dark ache would not give up its hold on her heart. She was dying inside. Yes, she desperately needed to get away.

Anton's 215-foot mini-cruise ship was moored for boarding at the Las Brisas Yacht Club on Long Beach Marina. Followed by a burly porter with her bags, Trish descended a ramp to the dock and walked to the gangway, where a queue of glamorous passengers were boarding. Her awe at the size of Anton's ship was only surpassed by her awe at the sight of his "dearest friends." She spotted a well-known writer of lusty mysteries, an aging Broadway actress, a television soap-opera star and a notorious Hollywood agent.

Trish made her way to the top of the gangway, where Anton greeted her with a quick peck on the cheek. An exotic redhead who appeared to be Anton's appointed hostess directed her to the staterooms belowdecks.

After the porter left her bags, Trish shut her stateroom door, let out an excited sigh and sat on the bed.

A sudden burst of static made her jump. From an intercom above the bathroom door, the skipper introduced himself and announced they would be departing shortly. He invited everyone to the promenade deck for a bon voyage cocktail party.

Was she really on her way to Cabo San Lucas with a shipful of prominent people? Feeling a little overwhelmed, she decided to skip the cocktail party and rest in her room awhile before venturing into such a sophisticated crowd.

She read for a while and tried to nap, but a familiar sadness began to crowd in on her, and in the quiet of her stateroom there seemed no way to avoid it. Hoping the other guests were still at the cocktail party, she slipped on a new Spandex one-piece bathing suit, and headed for the swimming pool on the upper deck.

Trish sighed contentedly and rolled over on her stomach to bake. After an uninterrupted hour of poolside sunshine, she realized Anton had been wise to invite her. She felt replenished already. Even the dark ache around her heart had lightened a bit. By the time they got back, she would be full of creative urges again—fairly bursting to paint. And she hadn't thought about Zach once . . . until now.

Damn—those ice blue eyes and tousled blond curls swept into her thoughts before she could squeeze them out. And to make things infinitely worse, she saw him as he was that first night when the towel dropped away— sinewy and golden and built like a stallion. . . . Oh Lord!—she tried to suppress the image, but a vibrant stab of excitement made her stiffen. A feverish flush burned across her skin. Zach Tanner, she warned silently, I left you back in L.A.—now stay there!

She was still struggling with her memories when the skipper announced that dinner would be at 6:00 P.M. in the mid-deck dining room, followed by big-band dancing on the aft deck. She gathered up her things, took a stairway to the main deck and walked out to the ship's bow. Soft waves sliced against the hull, but the soothing sounds did little for her frustration.

The attraction to Zach is only physical, she told herself. It's like hot fudge sundaes. Once you give them up, you lose your taste for them—right?

Wrong. A neon sign flashed. *Wrong.*

A shuddery sigh escaped her as the dark ache reclaimed her heart. She couldn't deny it any longer. It was more than chemistry, much more. She longed to see him, hear his voice . . . touch him. Just to be with him, to feel his reassuring warmth, his arms around her again. Oh, please, she pleaded silently, just once more, if only for a moment. . . .

A tremor shook her. It crumbled her restraints and freed a swell of sadness. The loss has nearly crippled me, she realized. I can't paint; I can't think; I'm barely functioning.

How could she hurt this way for a man she'd known so briefly? But she did . . . oh, she did. In her best moments she felt nothingness. In her worst moments she felt as though someone had taken her off life support and left her to die. *God help her, she hurt.* "Oh, Zach—" She whispered broken words into the wind. "Why did you force me to make a choice?"

Her heart thudded painfully. *Why?*

The question reverberated until suddenly she knew she didn't care. She didn't even care why. At this moment, she would give anything, *anything* to be with him. Only he could relieve this pain, only he could make her whole. . . .

Stop this, Trisha, a voice warned. Don't let it happen again. Don't let yourself love him. *Don't go back.* . . .

You won't survive this time, it whispered. *You won't survive.*

Tears welled up and spilled over.

A blustery head wind made her hair fly like a dark flag.

On the horizon, a clear china-blue sky and a sculptured coastline stretched forever.

The dancing had already started by the time Trish reached the aft deck at nine that evening. Swing music, festive lanterns and garlands of sparkling lights gave the area a ballroom atmosphere. She stood by a ribbon-draped railing where she could watch the graceful dancing and listen to the soft swish of water below. After a time, the dulcet rhythms worked their magic on her wounded spirit, and she began to feel a soothing, healing stillness.

You know the thrill of escaping to a world of **PASSION...SENSUALITY ...DESIRE...SEDUCTION... and LOVE FULFILLED...**

Escape again…with 4 FREE novels and

get more great Silhouette Desire novels —for a 15-day FREE examination— delivered to your door every month!

Silhouette Desire offers you real-life drama and romance of successful women in charge of their lives and their careers, women who face the challenges of today's world to make their dreams come true. They are not for everyone, they're for women who want a sensual, provocative reading experience.

These are modern love stories that begin where other romances leave off. They take you *beyond* the others and into a world of love fulfilled and passions realized. You'll share precious, private moments and secret dreams…experience every whispered word of love, every ardent touch, every passionate heartbeat. And now you can enter the unforgettable world of Silhouette Desire romances each and every month.

FREE BOOKS

You can start today by taking advantage of this special offer— the 4 newest Silhouette Desire romances (a \$9.00 Value) *absolutely FREE,* along with a Mystery Gift. Just fill out and mail the attached postage-paid order card.

AT-HOME PREVIEWS FREE DELIVERY

After you receive your 4 free books and Mystery Gift every month you'll have the chance to preview 6 more Silhouette Desire romances—*before they're available in stores!* When you decide to keep them you'll pay just \$11.70, (a \$13.50 Value), *with no additional charges of any kind and no risk!* You can cancel your subscription at any time just by dropping us a note. In any case, the first 4 books and Mystery Gift are yours to keep.

EXTRA BONUS

When you take advantage of this offer, we'll also send you the Silhouette Books Newsletter free with every shipment. Every informative issue features news on upcoming titles, interviews with your favorite authors, and even their favorite recipes.

Get a Free
Mystery Gift, too!

**EVERY BOOK YOU RECEIVE WILL BE
A BRAND-NEW FULL-LENGTH NOVEL!**

Escape with 4 Silhouette Desire novels (a $9.00 Value) and get a Mystery Gift, too!

Silhouette ❤️ Desire®

Silhouette Books, 120 Brighton Rd., P.O. Box 5084, Clifton, NJ 07015-9956

Yes, please send me FREE and without obligation, the 4 newest Silhouette Desire novels along with my Mystery Gift. Unless you hear from me after I receive my 4 FREE books, please send me 6 new Silhouette Desire novels for a free 15-day examination each month as soon as they are published. I understand that you will bill me a total of just $11.70 (a $13.50 Value), with no additional charges of any kind. There is no minimum number of books that I must buy, and I can cancel at any time. The first 4 books and Mystery Gift are mine to keep, even if I never take a single additional book.

NAME _____

(please print)

ADDRESS _____

CITY _____ STATE _____ ZIP _____

SIGNATURE (if under 18, parent or guardian must sign). _____

CT 1835

A waiter came by with a tray of drinks. She took a club soda and sipped it slowly. Glancing about the dance floor, she saw that a number of the dancing couples had disappeared. Besides herself, there were only a half-dozen couples left on the deck. Where was Anton, she wondered, and everybody else?

An hour later, Trish had had enough. She'd danced several times and her partners were pleasant enough, but she felt restless. Should she go to her stateroom and read? Or explore the rest of the ship in search of the other guests? Deciding a walk might bring her out of the doldrums, she chose the latter. One of her dancing partners had told her there was a private salon belowdecks where some of Anton's friends would be congregating.

Figuring the noise would lead her to the private salon, she descended to the lower deck. Two hulking men stood just outside a stateroom door. She recognized one as the porter who had carried her bags. The other looked suspiciously like a nightclub bouncer.

She approached them and smiled. "I was told there was a party on this deck?"

Aware that her breasts were substantially bared in the white strapless evening gown she wore, Trish nevertheless resisted an impulse to cover herself as the bouncer's eyes roamed over her.

"Party?" she repeated.

The muscle-bound porter grinned foolishly. "Sure," he said. "Your place or mine?"

"I was asking a question," she enunciated slowly. "Where's the party?"

The other man interceded. "Your name, ma'am?"

She told him, and he disappeared inside the private salon. A moment later he reappeared. "Sorry—it's a private party."

Trish held her ground. "I'd like to speak to Anton."

"Mr. Gregory's not in there right now, and I have orders not to admit anyone."

"Where can I find Mr. Gregory?" she pressed.

"He's in his stateroom and doesn't wish to be disturbed."

Her curiosity piqued, Trish persisted. "You don't understand. I'm Mr. Gregory's special guest. He's given me free run of the ship."

As the men looked at each other hesitantly, she brushed past them with all the aplomb she could muster, opened the door and stepped into a spacious room. So this was the private salon? The furnishings consisted of armless sofas, modular couches in various shades of pink and several cocktail tables. A self-serve bar, lavishly stocked with liquor, spanned half of one wall.

Rock music pounded from speakers recessed in the walls, and guests milled about drinking, laughing and yelling to be heard over the noise. In the room's center on a raised dance floor, the blonde, buxom soap opera star, obviously tipsy, was dancing with abandon.

Trish sighed and decided she preferred the party upstairs. Turning back to the door, she spotted Anton's European models, Jacques and Avril, dancing frenetically. Strange—she hadn't noticed them among the boarding party this morning. But no wonder; she hardly recognized them fully dressed.

As her fingers touched the doorknob, a drumroll came over the speakers and strobe lights flickered wildly. A muscular young man darted onto the stage and deftly edged the soap opera star from the spotlight. He wore a one-piece jumpsuit and looked exactly like one of those male exotic dancers she'd seen on TV.

Fascinated, Trish turned to watch for a moment. He danced like a professional—twisting, turning, gyrating to every pulse of the music. Eyes widening, she saw his hand flash up and unzip the jumpsuit. He slithered out of it like a snake shedding its skin. The crowd roared and applauded. Wearing a pair of athletic shorts beneath, he picked up the jumpsuit, twirled it over his head and let it fly. Trish saw it coming and tried to dodge, but the suit ended up draped over her shoulder as if she'd planned it that way.

A raucous cheer erupted from the crowd. She smiled and flushed, then gingerly picked the suit off herself and dropped it on the nearest chair. Turning back, she saw the shorts sailing her way and caught them automatically. What did he take her for? A clothes rack? Only the fear that she might encourage him stopped her from flinging the shorts back.

The revelers went crazy. "Take it all off!" they urged the dancer.

"Later," he laughed. "Right now I want to know which one of you ladies is coming up here to dance with me?" Throughout the crowd, feminine hands shot up. Cries of "me, me!" filled the air. The dancer's mind-boggling hip movements drew Trish's reluctant attention to the remainder of his outfit—a stretchy pink bikini.

Take it *all* off? Trish gulped nervously. They didn't do *that* on TV. As the women clamored to be chosen, Trish saw the dancer's eyes sweep over the crowd. Tossing the shorts on the chair, she edged toward the door again.

"Where's the foxy lady who caught my clothes?" he yelled. "She's the one I want!"

All eyes turned to Trish.

"Uhhh . . . she left," Trish bluffed nervously.

"Come on up here, sweetheart," he urged. "I won't bite."

"Thanks"—she shook her head—"but maybe another time? I really should be going—"

"I think she's playing hard to get," the dancer laughed, starting off the stage toward her. The crowd rooted madly.

She made a dash for the door and twisted the handle. Oh Lord—it's locked, she realized. Turning around, she saw the soap opera star edge into the dancer's path. "I'll dance with you, big guy," the tipsy actress offered. He had no chance to protest as she whirled him around and danced him back to the stage with great gusto.

Grateful for the diversion, Trish concentrated on finding a way out. There didn't appear to be another door.

Just then, the crowd's uproarious laughter made her head snap up in time to see the male dancer leaping from one tabletop to another. The blonde actress followed right behind him as a group of cheerleaders urged her on. Shouts of encouragement and shameless suggestions peppered the air.

The noisy room was getting smaller and hotter by the second. Music pounded from the speakers. Gripped with a spurt of claustrophobia, Trish pressed against the door. This bunch was fit for straitjackets! She had no doubt they'd be swinging from the chandeliers if there were any. It's time to make your exit, Trish, she resolved.

Twisting around, she tried the handle again and pounded on the door. "Open up!" she yelled. Muffled sounds came from the other side of the door, but it didn't open. "Open this door!" she demanded, pounding until her fists hurt. Still the door didn't budge.

When she turned back, a familiar form danced into her line of vision, and Trish felt the warm rays of hope. *Avril.* Maybe she knew a way out? But Trish's optimism paled as she watched the French model dancing and flirting madly with a tall, lanky cowboy. Avril's rapt admirer sported a Stetson, chaps and a wicked-looking mustache.

What's happened to Jacques? Trish wondered. With a darting glance, her question was answered. The male half of Anton's modeling team stood brooding by the bar.

Jacques's eyes darkened as he watched Avril's flagrant shenanigans. Angrily stubbing out his cigarette, he straightened and clenched a fist. Trish felt her heart rate quicken. Jacques looked about ready to start something, and the rest of the partygoers were just itching for a fracas.

"Jacques, don't do it!" Trish cried as she rushed to intercept his angry stride toward Avril and the cowboy. "There'll be a riot," she warned him, snagging his arm. "People will be hurt!"

"Believe it," Jacques snarled without a trace of a French accent. He jerked away and pushed through the throng. Breath held, Trish watched him collar the cowboy, and quickly closed her eyes. I've got to stop this, she realized, thinking desperately.

An idea so crazy it frightened her occurred. Could she? Should she . . . ?

An outraged shriek—Avril or the cowboy?—forced her decision.

A wastecan sat next to the wall by the bar. Trish found a book of matches on the counter, then quickly pressed the trash down in the can with the toe of her shoe. She didn't want a major fire, just a bit of smoke.

Poised to strike a match, she said a prayer, then hesitated. No, she couldn't do it, *not in a crowded roomful of people.*

A millisecond later, she witnessed the matches being whisked from her fingers and looked up just as the blonde actress struck one, lit the male dancer's cigarette with an outrageous wink and dropped the still-burning match into the can.

The refuse ignited like a flambé dessert. Horrified, Trish realized the wastecan had been used as a repository for half-finished glasses of liquor.

She dashed back to the door, pounding and screaming "fire!" Glancing back, she saw the curtains smoking like blue thunder. Maybe they were fire retardant? "Fire!" she screamed again. The door opened a crack. "Get an extinguisher," she blurted. "There's a fire in here!"

A minute later, the door burst open, and the porter rushed in with an extinguisher. "Where do I plug this in?" he said helplessly. Good grief, Trish thought, grabbing it away. She turned it right side up, found a pin and released it. Foam sprayed the room. "Wow!" someone cried, "whipped cream!"

Jacques and the cowboy scuffled past, and Trish iced them like a cake. Then, aiming the nozzle for the wastecan, she thrust the extinguisher at the porter and made a run for the open stateroom door.

"Hey," the other guard barked as she darted out the door and headed down the corridor, "where're you going?"

Afraid he might follow, she swerved down an adjoining corridor. At the first stateroom door, she peeked in, saw the room was empty and slipped inside. Shutting the door quietly behind her, she waited. As soon as the coast was clear, she'd try to find Anton. Did he know his guests were turning the ship into a floating free-for-all?

An odd growling noise caught her attention. She looked about the dimly lighted stateroom, then saw a glow coming from under the bathroom door. Someone was in there!

The bathroom door swung open, and the exotic redhead, wearing blue satin men's pajama tops, undulated out and draped herself on the round bed. Great, Trish moaned to herself, now how do I get out of here? She stifled a gasp as Anton appeared in the doorway wearing the bottom half of the pajamas.

"Ma chérie." He leered at the redhead.

"Oh, Anton," she purred back. "Come to me now." Pursing her lips, she coaxed him. "Quickly, quickly!"

Anton's eyes glazed over. As he moved toward the bed, Trish looked away.

Reaching behind her, she tried desperately to find the doorknob. A movement to her left caught her eye. She froze, pressing against the wall as the wardrobe door opened slightly. In the shadows of the closet she saw a man. A crew member, she realized by his clothing. Was everybody weird around here? Even the crew? He crept out of the closet, focused a camera on the half-dressed couple and began snapping pictures furiously. Either they didn't hear him, or they didn't care. More likely the latter, she decided. After witnessing tonight's debacle, nothing on this pleasure barge would surprise her.

At that moment, the crew member turned and saw her.

Silver eyes flashed.

Trish screamed. The weirdo with the camera was Zach Tanner!

9

Trish's scream split the air. Anton, poised to leap onto the bed, froze like a wax-museum figure. Struggling to get up, the startled redhead rolled off the bed and thumped to the floor at Anton's feet.

Zach hesitated a fraction of a second, then lowered the camera into its shoulder case and came straight for Trish.

"You?!" she gasped, backing up. "What are you doing here? With a camera? Taking pictures?"

He grabbed her wrist. "Come on—let's get out of here. *Now!*"

She jerked free. *"Taking pictures?* My God! You're as weird as everybody else around here!"

"Let's go!" Zach whispered harshly. He pulled Trish back, flung the door open and gave her a vigorous boost into the corridor. Before she had her balance, he had a tight hold on her forearm and was propelling her toward the outer deck.

He stopped long enough to check the adjoining

passageway, and she took advantage of his loosened grip to wrench free. "I'm not going anywhere with a picture-snapping peeping tom!" she asserted indignantly.

"You think I was in that closet just for kicks?" He snorted, an angry laugh. "Sorry, but watching Gregory in action is not my idea of fun."

Behind them, Anton appeared in the doorway, apparently recovered from his initial shock. "Guards! Guards!" he squalled.

From down the adjoining corridor, the porter appeared, covered in foam, still gripping the spewing fire extinguisher. Clouds of blue smoke wafted from the room. Next the bouncer pushed out. Anton stumbled toward them. "Get that man!" he screamed, pointing at Zach. "Take his camera!"

The porter dropped the fire extinguisher and ran for Zach.

Zach nimbly sidestepped, and the porter, unable to stop, plowed full on into the corridor wall. With a well-placed chop between the shoulder blades, Zach dropped him to the floor, then dusted off his hands and grinned.

He's actually enjoying this, Trish thought, horrified, as the bouncer hurtled himself like a human missile just as Zach started to turn back. The camera case went flying. Hulking arms wrapped around Zach from behind. The two men crashed to the floor and rolled across the corridor. Jumping to his feet, the bouncer poised himself to kick Zach viciously in the ribs.

With a gasp, Trish leapt for his kicking foot. She caught it on the downswing. Startled, he swayed like a skyscraper in an earthquake. Zach flashed to his feet, planted a fist in the skyscraper's middle and stood back to watch him topple. The passageway walls trembled.

Sprawled on the floor, her hands still locked around the bouncer's ankle, Trish looked up.

Zach grinned expansively. "Does this mean you care?"

She grimaced and struggled to her feet. "Don't get your hopes up. I lost my head."

At the far end of the corridor, Anton sniffed the air like a retriever. Following the trail of blue smoke, he stopped in horror at the open doorway to the private salon. "Fire!" he shrieked. "My ship's on fire!"

"No—!" Trish called to him, afraid the man would die of heart failure. "It's not your ship, Anton. It's just a wastecan—"

The male dancer, layered in foam, burst through the door and fled down the corridor past Trish and Zach. A moment later, the soap opera star stumbled out. "Where is he?" she gurgled, his athletic trunks tucked in her bodice.

Trish felt Zach's hand grip her upper arm. "Let's get out of here," he urged.

"No!" she protested, twisting out of his grasp. Was she any safer with him than with the lunatics on this boat? Maybe she should jump overboard and swim for it? The social life of killer sharks seemed preferable to this.

Zach grabbed his camera case, and then, before Trish knew what was happening, she was being slung over his shoulder like a potato sack. Bouncing wildly, she hung on for dear life as he sprinted up the stairs to the boat deck.

"Put . . . me . . . down," she cried feebly, as he bounded to the ship's side and then called out to someone below. A moment later she felt his hands span her waist and rib cage, gripping so hard she could barely breathe. Lifting her like a rag doll, he held her over the side of the ship.

He's throwing me overboard! she thought in terror. And then her feet came in contact with something solid. "It's the boarding ladder," he said brusquely. "Put your feet on the steps, grab the railing and climb down. There's a speedboat below."

The thunder of footsteps and Anton's screams of "find him!" assaulted her ears. The bouncer burst through the doorway onto the deck.

"*Go!*" Zach yelled at her.

She went. God only knew why, but she went.

The boat sped away. Trish huddled near the bow, Zach's leather jacket wrapped around her. The roar of the outboard motor muffled all other sounds, even Anton's high-pitched screams.

A swarthy mustached man, his hair covered with a fisherman's cap, was at the boat's steering wheel. Trish stared out over the bow into blackness. She could see nothing, no other boats, no sign of shore. Apprehension stirred in the pit of her stomach. Where were they taking her?

Icy wind stung at her face and blew her hair into wild dark tangles. When she tried to hold it back, loose strands broke free and snapped against her cheeks like tiny whips. Pulling the jacket tight, she turned guardedly and looked back at Zach.

His body tense and expectant, he sat at the stern, twisting around frequently to glance back at the receding ship. He thinks they're going to come after us, she realized with a shiver of fear.

The night's craziness caught up with her all at once. What was happening? Why had Zach been on the ship? In Anton's stateroom? Taking pictures? Her mind resisted the possibility of perversion. Zach was no voyeur; firsthand experience made her reasonably sure of that. He was a doer, not a watcher. Vital, virile, all male. . . .

Her stomach tightened. Stop remembering, Trish, she moaned silently. Smarten up, girl—there's something very ominous going on here. What is Zach Tanner up to? What does he want?

The answer hit her like a blow. He intends to blackmail Anton! To extort money from him! Why else would he take that kind of picture? A lump lodged in her throat. She tried to swallow and couldn't. She wouldn't have believed he was that sort of man. What did she know about him really? she thought, a little hysterically. *What did she know about this reckless man who'd just abducted her?*

Her breathing went shallow as she watched him.

Intense and preoccupied, he stared out over the water, his features fierce with determination. An aura of kinetic energy surrounded him. Moonlight shimmered through his hair like silver fire. What have you done, Zachary Tanner? she asked silently, urgently. *Who are you?*

As though aware of being watched, he swung full around to look at her, his eyes glinting. His jaw moved imperceptibly. The pale scar constricted. Vibrant fear and excitement shot through her. Oh, God help her— she didn't care. She wanted to be here—with him.

No matter what—she wanted to be with him.

She stiffened protectively. What kind of emotion could survive such fears and suspicions? What was his hold on her?

The outboard's engine slacked off, idling as the driver pulled the boat into a dock. What now? she wondered nervously. She didn't even know if they were in the United States. Had Anton's ship crossed the Mexican border at some time during the evening? Fear nudged again. The possibility that she was out of the country— far from everything she knew and understood—only magnified her insecurity.

Zach stood up, stepped out onto the dock and threw a line around a cleat, securing the boat's stern. Unmoving, she watched him.

As the driver secured the bow, Zach reached out to help her up on the dock. As his hand pressed hers, the contact set her nerves on edge. She avoided looking at him. Silly, she chided herself; but avoiding those silver eyes helped her to hold onto what little strength she had.

"This way," he said, gesturing the length of a creaky,

dimly lit ramp that led off the dock to a small houseboat. Crickets crooned and fireflies darted, showering the darkness with sparks.

"Zach, where are we?"

"Just south of Tijuana—"

The dock rolled again as the swarthy man jumped onto it and approached. "Thanks, Manuel," Zach said, pulling some bills from his pocket and pressing them into the man's hand.

As Manuel turned and walked away, Trish experienced a premonition of danger. She wanted to cry out and stop him. Her heart beating faster, she watched as he disappeared up the dock. The night was uncannily still. Even the crickets quieted, accentuating the sense of isolation. They were alone. *She was alone.*

Zach touched her arm and she nearly screamed. "We'd better get going," she blurted. "It's a long drive home."

"We're not going home," he said, looking into her frightened eyes. "We're going to get some things settled before we go anywhere—" He took her arm and led her toward the ramp. At the bottom, she halted.

"Wait a minute. Settle what things? Don't I have any say in this? What if I want to go home *right now?*"

"Well . . ." He paused. "If Manuel had a telephone in his houseboat, and if you were feeling *very* brave, you could call a Tijuana taxi, but since he doesn't . . ." He shrugged, letting the words trail off.

Her paranoia shot for the stars as she realized she had brought nothing with her. No bags, no purse, *no money.* She had the clothes on her back—a slinky, strapless evening gown—and nothing more. She was in a foreign country without money or resources, accompanied by a man of suspicious character with whom she felt burgeoning fear, wild desire and precious little control. *She was a sitting duck!*

Her thoughts twisted frantically. Wait—had he said *Manuel's* houseboat? She grabbed for the straw. "How can we settle anything with Manuel hanging around?" she said desperately. "We'd have more privacy in a car. I vote we drive home. We'll talk on the way."

He shook his head, walked up the ramp to the houseboat, and pushed open the door. "Manuel's gone—and well paid for his absence. We'll have total privacy."

After peering tensely through the open door, Trish brushed past him, entered the houseboat and went straight to a round wooden table. Pulling out one of the straight-backed chairs, she perched on it rigidly. Her eyes took in the narrow room—a combination living-dining area, sparsely decorated and surprisingly tidy. At the far end was a doorway. A bedroom? she wondered nervously.

Zach shut the door and bolted it. She watched and saw him hesitate, his hands still on the locks, his back to her. A cord in his neck tightened. When he turned, his face was taut with indecision. The room vibrated with silence. She heard her own heart thudding.

With a sigh, he began to pace the room like an enclosed animal. Tiny pricks of fear and excitement assailed her. She remembered that night in her beach house—his tanned, sinewy body striding across the room in a black bikini, her body tensing with every flex of muscle.

He turned toward her. His eyes sparkled like diamonds—hot, blue-white, multifaceted. She stiffened. Did he know he was sending shock waves of sexual energy her way? Did he feel her sharp anticipation—and her desire—despite the fear?

"Listen," he said with gruff abruptness. "I know I'm going to regret this, but there's something I have to tell you about me—"

Anxiety gripped her. Something he *had* to tell her? Why didn't she want to hear it? *No.* Whatever it was she couldn't let him tell her. *Not now.* She was with him again, after days of deprivation, and she couldn't face another painful choice. She wanted to be with him despite fear—no matter how crazy or reckless it was. She couldn't risk hearing anything that might split them apart.

"What happened on the boat—" he started.

"No! Don't tell me—"

He hesitated, perplexed. "Mac, don't stop me now. I have to—"

She raised her hands. "Shut up, Zach! I don't want to hear it."

He looked startled. "Did you say *shut up?*"

She took a deep breath and stood up. "Yes."

His face was a mask of shock and puzzlement. "But it concerns Gregory, too—"

It took all her courage, but she walked to him, her heart pounding, and stared up into his eyes. "I don't care."

A moment hung in time as they looked at each other. His face was open, expectant, urgent in its confusion. His eyes were hard and soft at once. She was gripped with longing . . . with a vibrant desire to know the feel of his arms, his mouth, his sweet, hard body again.

He watched her, perplexed, enthralled. His voice clotted. "You don't care?"

"I don't care if you're a blackmailer. I don't care what your plans are for Gregory—I just don't care." She reached up with trembling fingers and touched the corner of his mouth where the lips narrowed and came together, soft, yet taut.

A dazzling sensation swelled and spiraled through her. She was bursting with longing! "I'm dying from need of you," she whispered hoarsely. "I can't think about anything but you." Her fingers found his lips. "This incredible mouth." Her hands fluttered over his shoulders and down. "These warm arms, these searching hands—how they make me feel."

His face contorted. He struggled for control. "Mac— stop. Let me tell you first."

No, *no!* He wouldn't tell her anything. Rising up on her tiptoes, she kissed him lightly, fiercely. With both hands, she pulled his shirt free from his jeans, then slipped her fingers underneath and felt the leanness of his waist, the muscled rib cage and the soft, sensuous thicket of chest hair. His nipples hardened as she found them.

"Oh, no," he groaned. She felt his muscles ripple as a tremor racked him. "Mac, what are you doing to me . . . ?" His words became a rasping whisper as he pressed his palms to her temples and raised her face to his. "Mac? Oh, baby—won't you let me tell you first—?"

"No—" She barely got the word out before his mouth silenced her. Sounds of anguish and desire came from within him as he gripped her arms and kissed her. The impact held such intensity she lost touch with everything but his lips and the hands that locked her in place.

"I don't know what to do about you," he murmured, his voice bristling with passion. "I'm a stick of dynamite, lady—and you just lit the fuse." His fingers tangled in her hair as he searched her face. "What do you want from me?"

The word caught in her throat, then broke free in a husky, breathless rush. "You."

A smile flickered across his face like candle flame. "You got it," he said hoarsely.

Before she could move he nudged her up against the wall. "The bedroom's too far away," he breathed.

She looked up at the desire in his eyes and felt jagged streaks of excitement. "Yes"—she nodded, her voice odd and trembly—"too far."

"Turn, Mac," he ordered shakily, "turn around."

She did, her heart beating wildly.

As he lifted her hair, his lips found the back of her neck, then brushed down over the jutting bone of her shoulder blade and into the hollow between. He began to unzip the white evening gown slowly. Ever so slowly. What have I done? she thought, shivering violently at the light pressure of his hand as it moved down her back. As the dress loosened, she remembered that she was wearing only panties underneath. "Mac," he whispered, his breath hot, "I need to touch you—" His hand stopped in the arch of her back. The dress slipped from her body and dropped to the floor.

She looked down at her own nakedness. Barely able to breathe, she saw his hands span her hipbones, and then felt them pull her against him. As her back came into contact with his fully clothed body, a flush heated her skin. One of his hands slid to her stomach and flattened, pressing palm down; the other brushed over her rib cage and found her breasts. Exhaling with a sharp gasp, he cupped and caressed and molded the full, silky ovals to his hungry touch.

"Zach?" she breathed aloud, frightened by the sheer riot of arousal his touch generated.

With a tight sound of frustration, he wrapped his arms around her and swept her up hard against him. Just as quickly, he eased his hold.

"Easy, baby, easy," he whispered, "it's all right." His hand spanned the side of her neck and jawline as he turned her head slightly, until his lips found and caressed the sensitive outer edge of her mouth. It was tender, exquisite, powerfully erotic. A flash of pure desire erased any remnants of fear. She arched her body spontaneously, wanting to turn to him.

"Wait, baby, not yet," he moaned, his voice roughened and emotional. "I lose control with you, Mac, *I lose control*. No one has ever made me feel the way you do." His fingers feathered across her skin, finding her silky thighs, stroking upward to her femininity.

Again, she arched to turn, to hold him, to taste his sweet mouth, but he held her firm. "Wait, Mac, let me cool down so I can make it good for you," he said, his voice a throaty growl. "Wait—just a little longer." With husky promises of passion, he moved, pressing his heated body against her back. The rough fabric of his jeans teased her soft skin; his hardness urgently aroused her. A deep, dazzling sensation accelerated her breathing. I need him too much, she thought desperately. The man is a demon. He makes me wait. He makes me want him beyond anything else. Desire beat within her, pushing for release. From a tiny center of sensation a brilliant ache pulsed, inflaming her need, weakening her limbs.

"Turn around, Mac, turn—" he groaned.

She did, urgently. His demon hands reclaimed her breasts. Fingers trembling, she reached to unsnap his jeans.

With a startled moan, he gripped her shoulders, then brushed down the sides of her body to her hips. His thumbs pressed into the soft hollows of her pelvis.

"Oh God," he whispered, as her fingers brushed against his tight stomach muscles. "Hurry—"

The jeans joined her dress on the floor and their underwear followed. He kicked the clothes aside, swept her into his arms and carried her to the sofa, pressing her down into the cushions with the force of his mouth and his body.

Breaking the pounding kiss, his breath caught in a husky, pleading moan. "Do you want me, Mac? Baby?" His hand found the pulse between her thighs. Through a sharp rush of longing she cried out.

It was all the answer he needed.

With sighs of desire, she let her hands ride over his body, stopping at his hips, gripping, her knuckles pressing white against his hipbones. Their fierce mutual passion had released her need; only the sweet hardness he possessed could relieve it. "Oh yes, now, Zach," she said, her words broken with rapid gasps, *"now."*

With a swift movement, he parted her thighs, positioning himself between them. The feel of him sent weakness spiraling through her, and she reached spontaneously to catch his shoulders. Corded muscles bunched beneath her hands.

As he thrust forward with slow, straining urgency, his hardness found her. With a wild, broken moan he pressed through her body's sweet resistance until he had entry.

Her fingers gripped and bit into his shoulders. Behind her closed eyes, a shower of sparks burst as he moved with fervent, ardent strokes. He was so warm, so deep, so good. The force of their joining thrilled her, completed her. She needed him, loved him . . . *loved him.* His energy, his strength, his vibrant body and pounding heart made her whole.

Her eyes flashed open to see his features constrict with passion. His need stormed her senses. His darkened eyes met hers, and an exchange of such naked wanting passed between them that she felt a rip of pain through her heart. Oh God, she *loved him.* The realization was so shattering, so beautiful, it was all she could do not to turn away.

His voice breaking, he whispered her name.

Tears stung her eyes. "Oh . . ." She struggled to say his name as he bent toward her.

The kiss took them deeper and deeper, penetrating layers of intimacy. Ragged sounds of emotion punctured the air, and the steady, urgent coming together of their bodies heightened and stretched pleasure to the breaking point.

"Are you mine, Mac?" he whispered finally, harshly. "Tell me, *tell me.*" His ardent, uncontrolled thrusts vibrated through her.

"Yes," she cried softly, again and again, as a vibrant wave of pleasure built. Sensations throbbed and beat and swelled as the wave crested high, then dropped to stream through her in surging rivulets.

Through a gauzy, shimmering veil, she felt his lips on her breast, pulling sensuously at a firm, quivering nipple. She felt him splay his hard fingers beneath her hips and move urgently and deeply within her. Again and again their glistening bodies met. A brilliant white light strobed around them as he strained and fought to hold back.

Against her mouth, he whispered his uncontrollable

passion before losing his voice to small, harsh groans and his body to short, shuddering thrusts. He pulled her close with strong, urgent arms and cried her name explosively. Carried by his turbulence, she felt a powerful wave build. Rills of pleasure lifted her as she surrendered to pure, sweet joy, riding the current, hanging onto him for dear life.

Through whispers of love, she felt the wave crest and break, streaming and bubbling out to her extremities in soft ripples. She called his name silently, repeatedly, holding him until her arms were so weak she had to let go.

Breathless, she floated languidly on the surface of sensation. With a small, ecstatic sigh, her body went luxuriously limp, and she sank back into the cushions of the sofa.

Unable to talk, or even to open her eyes, she lay in his arms and floated in a misty euphoria.

After a time, vaguely aware that he'd withdrawn, she felt herself being lifted and carried, then lowered to a bed. Stretching out languorously, she felt him lie next to her, brushing kisses on her closed eyes, her chin, her parted lips as he whispered how good she was, how much he needed her, how much he loved her . . . *loved her?*

Had he said that? Had she really heard that? Her eyes blinked open.

"Welcome back," he laughed softly. "I was beginning to feel a little left out."

"What did you say?" she asked urgently.

"I felt left out."

"No, no—before that."

He looked puzzled, then smiled. "Ohhh, you little rascal, you're fishing, aren't you? I told you how beautiful and utterly sensuous you are."

She was beautiful? and sensuous? Her heart lightened, but only momentarily. "Oh, damn, she *was* fishing, but not for compliments. Had he said he loved her? She couldn't ask. She just couldn't. Stubbornly, she decided she would believe he'd said it. At least for now.

Snuggling close and wrapping herself around him in a warm tangle of arms and legs, she lay still, listening to his heartbeat. A musky salt breeze carried through a partially open bedroom window. Outside, a resonant string symphony of crickets performed their soft, relentless night music.

After a time, she raised herself up on an elbow and marveled at the serenity of his face in repose. She felt a deep, endless ease. With a sign of contentment, she laid her cheek on his chest, her fingers ruffling the flaxen hair on his belly and then curiously exploring the graceful scar that pointed to his maleness. How had he sustained such an injury?

His remembered words disturbed her. "There's something I have to tell you about me." She ignored them until finally she couldn't anymore.

He lay with his arms folded behind his head, strangely silent. She touched his jawline and let her fingers travel to his cleft chin. "Tell me now, Zach."

Rolling his head, he looked at her. "Are you sure?"

She nodded. With a heavy sigh, he pulled away from her and sat up. She suddenly felt a need to cover herself.

Reaching to the foot of the bed, she pulled a flowered comforter up around herself and huddled in it, watching him. Whatever it is, she resolved, I can handle it.

He looked at her finally, and she felt the tension. "Listen," he said quickly, "I'm going to take a shower first—join me?"

She shook her head. How could he take a shower? He was procrastinating. That meant it was something bad. A cold sensation like an icy finger tapped at her stomach. Should she have let him tell her before . . . ?

Moments later he emerged from the steaming bathroom, wearing a short terry cloth robe. "Must be Manuels's," he said, looping the tie around his waist. The exposure of his long legs was somehow very sexy.

He sat on a chair next to the bed. She felt their separateness as if it were a tangible thing. Why were his eyes so gray and somber? She stiffened instinctively, anticipating pain.

"I'm not a taxi driver," he said quietly. "I'm a private detective assigned to investigate Anton Gregory."

Her mind took the information and assimilated it with efficient detachment. A private detective? Of course, that was why he kept turning up when she was with Anton, that was why he was taking pictures. Not a pervert, not a blackmailer—*a detective!* Oh, hallelujah! A detective! She smiled exultantly and bubbled, "Like Jim Garner? I always loved *The Rockford Files.*"

He seemed surprised at her reaction. "Mac—I'm serious. I don't think you understand—it's not just Gregory." He hesitated, his jaw tightening. "I'm investigating—"

"Who?" She smiled. This was exciting. Maybe she could help him solve the case. What had Anton done?

"You."

"Huh? What? Me . . . ?"

He leaned forward in the chair, his face taut with concern. "Your involvement with Gregory made you suspect, and I had to report it to my client's attorneys—they're running the investigation. After that, I was instructed to keep an eye on you as well."

"Me? You've been spying on me? Why?"

"My client plans to cite you as correspondent in a divorce action against Gregory."

"What—?" Her heart nearly stopped.

"My client is Lydia Hadding," he explained, "of the New York publishing family. She's also known as Mrs. Anton Gregory."

"But I—we—I mean Anton and I weren't lovers. I told you that! You said you believed me. Zach, my God, a divorce like that would be a vicious, messy scandal. It would hit every paper in the country. What are you trying to do to me?"

He stood up, riffling his hands through his wavy hair.

"I'm trying to get you out of this whole damn mess. That's why I told you to stay away from the guy. Mac, believe me, I had to do this—I have to get Gregory for several reasons. The attorneys have been pressuring me to nail him before he leaves for Europe. I was up against the wall." Muttering an expletive, he rubbed his forehead with his hand. "I boarded the boat thinking it was going to be *you* with Gregory—"

"Me?" she whispered, staggered. "But—but it wasn't me," she said defensively. "It was that redhead, and you've got pictures!"

"No," he sighed. "I'm afraid I don't. One of Gregory's thugs caught up with me as I was going over the side. In the scuffle I lost the camera overboard."

"Oh, no. Oh, Zach. How could you do this? Why didn't you tell me I was under investigation?"

His eyes pleaded, urging her to understand. "I told you everything I could. I'm a detective. Disclosing information on a case is unethical. I shouldn't be telling you now."

A strange fear chilled her. It felt like a cold echo from the past. Ethics? His professional ethics had stopped him from telling her what she was getting involved in? All the time he knew, yet never told her? What if she'd been with Gregory? What would he have done then? She was afraid to ask.

His eyes were sad and searching. "Mac, I've been struggling with myself since that night in the taxi—no, even before that. I wanted to tell you—"

"You should have, Zach. You owed me that, at least."

His head snapped back as if she'd slapped him. "I know," he said finally, softly, "I know." After a moment, he pushed himself from the chair and came to the bed. She pulled the blanket around her more tightly as he sat down. "Mac, there's more. There are other reasons I had to do what I did."

Her mind heard the words, but her heart didn't want reasons. It only knew she'd been under surveillance, *his* surveillance. Was that why he'd pursued her? Because of her link to Gregory? Was that why he'd wanted to be with her, why he'd made love to her?

She looked at him hesitantly. A tumult of emotions she couldn't define paralyzed her. He'd been investigating her? For how long? How much did he know about her? *Everything?*

10

Zach couldn't define the turmoil in her eyes, but he knew he saw pain there, and it gave him the answer to the dilemma he'd been struggling with since he met her. He should have told her, or he should have stayed away from her—totally away.

But God, he'd tried—twisted himself into knots trying.

Her small hands held the comforter tightly, defensively around her. "Why are you doing this, Zach? Spying on Anton? On me? Why?"

How much more should he tell her? Would it help if she knew? Maybe, he decided slowly, but not if she knew all of it. Only as much as necessary. "I told you, Mac. I'm a private investigator. I'm working for . . . his wife."

"If Mrs. Gregory wants a divorce," she questioned unsteadily, "why doesn't she just file for one?"

"She will—" He hesitated, caught by the dark,

shadowy beauty of her half-closed eyelids. She looked adorable bundled in that blanket. He wanted so much to touch her. "But . . . well, there are some sticky legal technicalities involved."

"Like what?" She looked up at him. Her eyes were soft, brown accusations.

He let out a heavy sigh and rubbed his jawline aggressively, then looked away. "I'm a damn fool, Mac. I should never have let you become involved. I should have found a way to stop you."

"You couldn't have stopped me," she said tonelessly, "but you should have told me."

Still facing away, he began. "Gregory's not the wealthy gallery owner he pretends to be—he's broke. Most of his galleries are mortgaged to the hilt, and he stands to lose everything because of the debts he's piled up." He half turned, glancing at her.

She was staring at him, her face pale with disbelief. Her hands had released the comforter and were frozen in small semifists.

"It's true," he said somberly. "The man has expensive habits—vices would be a better word. You got a little sampling on board his ship tonight."

"You mean in his stateroom?" she questioned. "The redhead?"

"That, and the party. Believe me, Mac, if you hadn't smoked them out, those friends of his would still be going strong. They were just getting started."

"But Anton wasn't there. Maybe he didn't know about the party?"

"Know about it? Oh, Mac, honey, he organized it. Gregory's private life is a three-ring circus. He should hire a barker and charge admission. Even when I figured out what was going on, I couldn't get any evidence. He keeps it all under wraps. Sophisticated security systems, hired guards, only a tight little group of friends involved."

"He's really broke?" she said slowly, as though trying

to cope with the idea. "Losing his galleries? How can that be?" Her throat constricted. "Why did you have to investigate him?" she asked hoarsely, looking up. "It's not necessary to show cause in California. If she wanted to divorce him, why didn't she just do it?"

Zach came back to the edge of the bed and sat. In addition to pain, he now read fear in her expression. Of course, he thought suddenly. Gregory holds the purse strings to her art career. If he folds, so does she.

With a needle prick of awareness, Zach realized he'd forgotten Mac's investment in all this. She had believed her dream was coming true, and in his hellish rush to get Gregory, he'd let her believe it. Why had he let it go this far? Why had he let this happen?

"Zach?"

She wanted answers, and dammit, Zach decided impulsively, she would get them, privileged information or not. Exhaling, he started. "At the time of her marriage to Gregory two years ago, Lydia Hadding insisted on a premarital agreement. Her first husband was a drinker and a skirt chaser. After she'd had her fill of gossip, she divorced him."

He paused, gauging Mac's reaction, aware that none of this would be easy for her to hear. She'd reclaimed her hold on the comforter and almost seemed to recede inside it.

Feeling a tug at his heart, he realized that he only had two options—telling her or not telling her—and either was equally cruel.

He continued finally. "In technical terms, the premarital agreement with Gregory stated that should either party commit adultery, the prior wealth and property that each brought to the marriage would no longer be subject to California's community property stipulations. In other words," he clarified quietly, "if Gregory strays and she catches him at it, he has no claim on her wealth when she divorces him."

"Is she very wealthy?" Mac asked, almost absently.

"Yes, *very*. Wealthy enough that half of her assets would bail Gregory out of his financial predicament and set him up in lavish style for the rest of his life."

"So that's why Anton is so careful to keep his affairs secret?" she asked pensively.

Zach nodded. "Lydia Hadding has suspected his double life for some time, but couldn't prove anything. I couldn't either—until tonight."

"And all along I was supposed to be the bait? Was that the plan?"

He felt as if she'd punched him in the stomach. She actually thought he'd set her up. "Mac—that isn't fair. I never wanted you to be involved. I asked you to stay away from him."

"But you've been investigating me—you said so." Her face was ashen. "For how long, Zach? What did you find out about me?"

"Nothing," he answered quickly, "except what you've told me yourself. I should have done a background check, but . . . I . . . I decided against it."

"Why?"

"I just couldn't do it," he admitted. Moving alongside her, he brushed her pale cheek with the back of his fingers. "I couldn't do it, Mac. I—we'd been together. We'd made love. There were feelings involved." He lifted her face with his hand, and the pain in her eyes stunned him. He'd expected anger, perhaps some hurt, but not this sheer pain. It tortured him. "Oh, baby," he said, voice catching, "I never meant to hurt you. God knows, I didn't. I was careless—preoccupied with what I had to do—I didn't think ahead. I didn't know it would come out like this. If I could go back and change it, I would. Believe me, Mac." He caressed her cheek, and the softness of her skin made him shudder. "You do believe me?"

She looked away.

His chest tightened. He shifted, stood and walked away. What did he do now? He couldn't tell her any more than he had. Then suddenly he knew . . . and it frightened him.

He turned, not quite able to catch his breath, and whispered, "Mac . . . I love you."

She looked up sharply.

He waited, his throat dry, his heart pounding. What was he doing? Was it true? Did he love her?

Her huge brown eyes searched his face, and then a wet tear pushed its way over her lower eyelid and caught in her lash before it dropped to her cheek. "Don't, Zach—" she said, her voice low and heartbreakingly sad.

"Oh God," he groaned, "it's true. It's true." He strode to the bed and took her hands. "I've never said that to a woman before. Please, baby, *please* believe me." Before she could say anything, he'd swept her into his arms and was cradling and rocking her like a child. "Somehow I'll make all this come out right, Mac, I swear it."

"Zach, stop," she repeated brokenly. But despite her words, she seemed to give in for a moment, letting her head drop into the curve of his neck.

As he reached to brush her hair back from her face, his fingers found wetness. A small river of tears streamed over her beautiful cheekbones. "Mac, don't—don't cry." He felt as if something were piercing his chest. "Hey, please, don't cry. It'll be all right, I promise."

But would it be? With that invisible umbilical cord tugging him in another direction? His chest ached relentlessly. Could he keep his promise?

She stiffened in his arms, and he held her tighter. "Easy, Mac," he coaxed, his voice hollow. "It'll all work out."

"Zach, don't," she pleaded softly, pulling out of his arms. "I need . . . I need to think . . . I . . ."

Twisting around, she tried to move away. He felt an impulse to laugh and cry all at once as she struggled with the comforter. It caught underneath her and pulled tight, half choking her as she attempted to crawl to the other side of the bed. She was so funny, so beautiful. He loved her.

He stood up to help her, but she shook her head, then scrambled around to rearrange herself. Finally, wrapped like a down-filled mummy, she huddled in a meditative state.

It seemed like forever before she finally peered at him from over the top of the comforter. "You love me?" she murmured, half thoughtful, half incredulous. "And Anton's broke. Sounds like a good news/bad news joke." She shrugged as she managed a wavery smile. "I guess this means I'm not going to be a famous artist."

"Yes, you are," he insisted. "You're talented. You'll make it without Gregory. Other gallery owners will show your work."

She shook her head sadly, resignedly. "Not after Anton goes down in flames and takes me with him."

"If Anton goes down in flames, he goes alone," he said firmly. His stomach knotted at the brash promise.

"And you, Zach Tanner—" Her eyes shimmered with uncertainty. "You say you love me. Can that be true?"

"I love you, Mac," he whispered hoarsely. "Cross my heart and hope to die."

"Oh Lord," she whispered to herself, "I wish that didn't frighten me so."

She looked like a child who wanted something desperately and, at the same time, like an adult who knew she couldn't have it. "Zach," she said, her voice barely audible. "I think it might have been better if you had investigated me. If you knew about me—everything—"

"What do you mean?" he cut in.

She turned away, her face buried in the comforter, and said something. It was muffled. She was trying to tell him something, but whatever it was, she wanted to hide from it. "Mac?" he said gently. "Honey? I can't hear you." Nearly disappearing inside the blanket, she continued talking.

"Hey," he repeated louder, beginning to chuckle. "I can't hear a word you're telling me. You're going to run out of oxygen in there, and don't count on me for CPR. Well . . . maybe a little mouth-to-mouth—"

Her head popped up then, and at the sight of her bright, sad eyes, his smile faded. "Baby, what's wrong? What is it?"

"I'm frightened. I can't help it, Zach. I'm frightened."

"Tell me what's frightening you. I'm here. I love you, Mac. I can help." He shifted closer.

Her head disappeared again. He backed off and waited quietly. Her head came up. "Oh, dear, I know this is silly," she admitted with a shaky sigh. "Just bear with me a minute, okay? While I work up my courage."

Finally, with a heavy sigh, she began. "I'm a woman with a past, Zach."

A woman with a past? Damn, but she was wacky and adorable.

She blinked and her eyebrows shot downward. "Are you smiling?"

"No." He shook his head and frowned vigorously to prove it.

"Yes, you were," she insisted. "I forbid you to smile while I'm baring my soul to you." She watched him, eyes narrowed, like a teacher calling for order.

He tried his Clint Eastwood frown.

"Okay," she said finally, pulling the blanket tight and looking down toward the foot of the bed. "I'm not kidding, Zach. My former life is a wrecking yard of emotional accidents. There are things you don't know about me. I've told lies and kept secrets, too. For starters, I've been married and divorced." She glanced at him quickly, checking his reaction.

He nodded, letting his face show no emotion. And in fact, he was only mildly surprised, even though he'd never thought of her as having been married. Somehow the image wasn't difficult to accept, but it made him curious. "Why didn't it work?" he asked.

"He left me," she said quickly, shortly.

That surprised him. "Left you? Why?"

She went on as though she hadn't heard the question. "We had great plans, he and I," she said with a sad smile, remembering aloud. "We met in college and married right after graduation. My major was art; his was business. We'd both planned to go on to graduate school, but money became a problem, so I took a job instead." Settling into her blanket, she looked as if she were slipping away. "As soon as he graduated we borrowed money—from the bank, from his parents and mine, from anyone who would make us a loan, actually —to open our own French country inn."

She glanced at Zach, a lingering, longing glance that baffled and thrilled him, and then she looked away. "You know the type of place I mean—French provincial cooking, bed and breakfast. Jerry—my husband—was odd, eccentric almost, in his passion for anything and everything French. I thought it charming at first. It attracted me. We had such plans, he and I." Her eyes closed briefly. "I loved him . . . energetically, I guess is the word. I was young then—I didn't know how to hold back. My love had no judgments, no reservations. It was full-out, everything I had to give. But even more than him, I loved *us*. Me and Jerry. What we were to become. We were going to be successful, he and I—at everything. Oh Lord, how many times he told me that—over and over. We talked and planned endlessly. Against all odds, we were going to make that elusive American Dream come true. Marriage, a French inn, a lovely home, two or maybe three moppets—" She stopped a moment and put her fingers to her lips. "Oh, yes . . . babies . . ." Her eyes misted. She shook her head quickly, determinedly, and then went on in a single-minded rush, as though trying to race ahead of her emotions.

"And of course I would have my painting, too. I was

quite a traditionalist in those days. I remember thinking myself so clever to have picked a career that would allow me to be home with my children. But of course all that would come later—the babies and my painting, I mean. We agreed, or rather Jerry insisted and I agreed, to wait until the inn showed a profit."

Her skin seemed pulled taut over her facial bones. Watching her, Zach had the feeling she was fighting back a surge of emotion.

"And two years later, when the inn was on solid ground," she continued rapidly, "he decided we should enlarge, so I kept my job. We enlarged the restaurant first, then later we added on more rooms. We got quite grand eventually, but somehow the time was never right for . . ." Her face suddenly lost its color and then regained it in an angry rush.

The American Dream was over, Zach realized.

"I found him in La Suite Bleue—," she said, her voice choked with biting irony, "so aptly titled."

After a tense moment, a self-deprecating smile twitched across her lips. "Fools rush in," she muttered, shaking her head. "I was so nervous and excited that day, and so frightened Jerry would be angry. I'd come to confess that I'd quit using birth control several weeks before and that I'd quit my job that morning. I felt so brave and purposeful—"

She almost seemed to flinch as pain narrowed and darkened her eyes. "The concierge told me a lady guest had called to complain about her suite's television, and Jerry had gone up to adjust the vertical pattern." Her face contorted as a brittle, faltering laugh forced itself through her lips. "By the time I found them, they were in a horizontal pattern. Needless to say, the only thing not turned on was the television. . . ."

With a small, explosive gasp, she began to laugh— that same brittle, heartrending laugh. Zach's temples ached as her eyes reddened, filled with tears. Struggling, her hands made small fists, and she clamored on, talking in short, rapid bursts, barely stopping to breathe.

"She was a French wine heiress. Beautiful, of course. Wealthy. And disgustingly *French*. "Zzzzhurrreee," she called him. He had the nerve to tell me she was helping him perfect his accent. He left the inn with her that night. In the morning he called and told me our marriage was over. He insisted on a quickie Mexican divorce. The next day I was a single woman. The next week he married her. God—" She threw her head back and looked up at the ceiling, her chin trembling. "I never really knew what hit me."

Angry tears streaked her cheeks. With a heavy, shuddering sigh, she lowered her head. "It was another month before I saw him again. With her, of course. I was at the back of a local antique store, trying to sell a French end table for enough to see me through until the divorce settlement came in, when they burst into the store, laughing and hugging. I was a mess, hair tied in a bandanna, my old raincoat—I wasn't in very good shape in those days. They nearly saw me before I got out. Oh God, I think that would have killed me. . . ."

Her voice faded to a soft, choking sound. "That same night I had a miscarriage."

He jerked forward in the chair.

She looked over at him, her face ashen and drawn tight, her eyes hollow, and murmured, "Not the easiest way for a woman to find out she's pregnant."

His heart twisted. "Mac—" he whispered.

She went on as though she hadn't heard him. "I spent a week in the hospital. The doctor said I was healthy as a horse, it was my mental state he was worried about. I told him I was fine. I thought I was. I felt nothing, no pain, nothing. He wasn't convinced, but he finally released me to go home that afternoon."

Her expression went glassy and vacant. "Funny," she said in a halting, faraway voice. "I've almost forgotten what happened next . . . seems like another lifetime . . . or another person . . . I was driving home when I saw a freeway entrance sign. I pulled to the right and started up the ramp—a long, curving overpass. I remember thinking it looked endless to me, long and sweeping and graceful. I was going fast, like the wind, and when I came to the curve the car didn't turn. I remember seeing the wall coming toward me and thinking, I have to turn now . . . but I didn't seem to have the strength . . . my hand didn't move . . . the car didn't turn. . . ."

Zach felt a surge of horror and nausea. He stood up, his body rigid.

"I saw the crash. I saw my car disintegrate in front of me. The hood, the engine exploded into fragments and then slowed, floating, hanging suspended there in the air. It was like watching a freeze-action frame. I remember waiting for the noise, but there wasn't any . . . and then from somewhere a low, rolling roar, like soft thunder. A deep, destructive sound, powerful, almost beautiful . . . maybe it was God's voice . . . but I could hardly hear it. It lifted me and shook me and shook me. . . ."

She quieted. Zach watched her, his gaze fixed and frightened.

Releasing the blanket, she let it fall loose, exposing her hands and arms. "When it let go of me, I remember falling back in the seat. I looked down and saw a cut on my arm. I remember thinking—my arm? Then, *my arm*—sort of possessively. That was my arm. *I was bleeding.*" She reached down and touched her forearm as though it had just happened. "Tha—," her voice broke, "that was the first time I knew it had happened to me."

An undiscernible emotion shook her, and she turned away. Feeling helpless, he watched her body convulse. When she turned back, her eyes were red-rimmed and brimming with tears. Her mouth stumbled to form words. "That cu . . . cut may have been small, Zach, but it stu . . . stung like fire—" Her fingers went to her trembling mouth as she struggled to smile. "And, oh, it gave me the mos . . . most incredible sense of being alive." Tears drenched her face. "B—by the time the par . . . paramed . . . by the time they got to me, I was laugh . . . laughing and sob . . . sobbing like a crazy woman."

Her sad, swollen eyes were alight with heartbreaking courage. But it was the sight of that small, wobbly smile on her tear-streaked face that undid him. He bolted around the bed and wrapped her in his arms. She shook and sobbed and wept.

Holding her in a fierce, protective embrace, he felt each wracking sob cut into him. Tears burned his eyes, and his throat locked shut in a painful spasm. It destroyed him to have her hurt this way. Holding her, loving her didn't seem to be enough.

She crumpled against his chest, her body surrendering to sharp gasps and long, shuddering sighs. He held her head with his hands, caressing her hair, holding her gently against him. "Oh, Mac," he whispered, barely able to speak. "Go ahead, cry it out, baby, let go of it."

It was a long time before she quieted enough to talk.

When she looked up at him, her face was soft and swollen and just beginning to regain its color. "I g— guess that was pr—pretty important," she said haltingly, blowing her nose with the tissue he'd given her. "I've cried so many times over losing him. But this was the first time I've cried over losing me."

"Hey," he breathed, relieved, smiling. "Hey, that's good, *that's great.*"

Her eyes brimmed with emotion, and a sigh slipped out as she touched his arm. "Thank you . . . for listening."

"Anytime," he said, his arms squeezing her bundled form tenderly. A warm silence surrounded their closeness for several moments before he asked, "Feel any better?"

After a thoughtful pause she nodded, murmuring "Yes, I do," and then pulled gently from his arms to sit next to him. Folding her legs Indian style, she arranged the comforter loosely around her. "The accident totaled my car," she said, sighing, "and I haven't driven since—that story I told you about the moving van was a fib. My arm healed with nothing more than some antiseptic and a bandage. The psyche took longer. To tell you the truth, I was a wreck, but at least I knew I wanted to live.

"There wasn't a lot of money when the divorce was finalized, but I took every cent of it, and then I went away. It felt so reckless, getting on a bus headed north, not even knowing where I was going. I wound up in Mendocino, a quiet, lovely little beach town. I stayed there for months, threw myself into painting, and eventually I began to heal. When I came back, I took the beach cottage in Playa del Rey and began to take art classes—"

"Sounds like a happy ending to me," he broke in gently.

"It might've been"—she shrugged—"if my money hadn't run out. I had that dream, Zach, that crazy dream to have an art career." The pace of her words accelerated as broken hopes were forced out. "It was in my blood, I wanted to be a working artist. Years of my life, everything I had went toward that goal. . . ." He sensed she was struggling to accept a past she couldn't change as she went on. "One day the money was gone, and I hadn't sold a single painting. I hadn't even managed to associate myself with a gallery. No prospects, *nothing to show for all that effort.*

"Dreams die hard, Zach." She nodded, pursing her lips as though to appear matter-of-fact about it all. "And mine went down fighting and screaming. Something deep within me refused to believe that I wasn't going to have what I'd worked so hard for; but when I couldn't beg, borrow or steal enough to make the mortgage payment, I had no choice. I took the only job I could get at the time—a clerk-typist position at Grover Chemicals

—and worked my way up from there. . . ." After an extended sigh, she looked over at him. "And I guess you know the rest of the story."

Yes, he knew the rest of the story. He knew he'd come into her life and fouled her dreams up again. And he knew beyond doubt that he was the last thing she needed then—or now.

"Oh, I almost forgot," she broke in suddenly, tremulously, her voice tinged with false lightness. "There is one other little fib I told you. . . ." Hesitating, she studied him for the space of a heartbeat, then shook her head. "No . . . enough is enough." Falling back on the bed, she rolled to her side, pulling her legs up like a weary, fragile child. "No more confessions tonight, okay?"

"Yeah, okay," he said, his chest aching at the fatigue in her face. Stretching out on his side, he faced her. Her eyes were so beautiful, so deep with hurt, and yet she smiled as if everything were going to be all right. "Do you understand now, Zach?" she asked softly, her dark eyes searching. "Why Anton was so important, why I couldn't let go of the opportunity he offered? My painting was the one thing I had left."

Those brown eyes haunted him. *Yes, he understood.* She's been to hell and back, he thought with a racking inner sigh, and all she wants is a chance for some happiness.

She reached over and touched the scar on his jaw. "I love you, Zach," she said quietly, "cross my heart." A moment passed before her beautiful eyes clouded over, dimmed with fear and distrust, and she pulled her hand away.

"But God help me, Zach, but I don't think I can stand to lose all my dreams again. Even if I can find another gallery to show my work, who will take me seriously as an artist if everyone believes I'm Gregory's mistress? And you—can I trust a man who's been using me for his own purposes all along?" The words broke off as her eyes sought his, probing clear to his soul.

He felt as though a fist were closing around his heart. His eyes stung with tears as he gathered her into his arms.

They came together in the night. Desperately, as if they both believed it would be the last time.

Just before dawn, she sleepily pulled herself from his arms and rolled over on her side, her back to him. As he moved close and covered her protectively with his arm, she edged back into the warm refuge of his body, snuggling and burrowing like a small animal seeking cover. With her slender, softly breathing form pressed close, he knew, in a way he never had before, how small she was and how strong she was, and how much he'd hurt her.

Careful not to wake her, he rolled over on his back and stared up at the ceiling. A ray of pale light crept through a crack in the window shade. It stretched across the room in a narrow quest. By the time it reached the foot of the bed, he knew. Now, Zach, *go now*—before she wakes.

He dressed quietly, wrote a note and put it on the pillow beside her. His arms ached as he resisted the impulse to hold her, even to touch her.

By the time he reached the California border, it was fully light. The air was crisp, and the sky clear, deep blue and hard as sapphires. A small seed of determination grew inside him. Was she up yet? he wondered, stopping the Plymouth for the border guard's cursory inspection. Had she read the note?

11

·~❀❀❀❀❀❀❀❀❀❀~·

Drowsy with sleep, Trish reached out and felt something soft. Only half realizing it was a pillow, she wrapped her arms around it and snuggled contentedly.

Recapturing a dreamy residue of glowing, gold-sprinkled landscapes and dulcet sounds, her arms stretched languorously. Her fingers brushed something on the bed. Hmmm . . . She felt it again lazily. Paper . . . ?

Unable to see with the pillow pressed against her face, she grasped the slip of paper in her fingers, then lost it. Rising up on an elbow, she pushed the pillow aside, opened one eye with great effort and watched the small, white rectangle float to the floor.

Where am I? she wondered, looking about the room. Oh, yes, the houseboat. Zach . . . ?

Her attention was drawn to the paper again. Something was written on it. Straining to see but too sleepy to get up, she hung over the side of the bed and read:

Mac, sorry to leave you this way, but I think I may be able to straighten this whole mess out. I've arranged for Manuel to drive you back whenever you're ready. Listen baby, it may take me a few days, but don't worry about *anything,* okay? Wait for me at your cottage. I love you, Mac, *I love you.* Cross my heart, Zach.

Tendrils of icy, foaming surf crawled up the beach's sandy incline and curled around Trisha's bare toes. She shivered, but didn't move. The water receded, gathered momentum and tickled her toes again.

The cruise, Mexico, the houseboat—it all seemed a dream now that she'd been home several days. Slipping her hands in the pockets of her cable-knit sweater for warmth, she felt the note beneath her fingers and remembered her reaction when she'd first read it. Her sleepy eyes had blinked, then sprung open. One line had stood out like a headline: "I think I may be able to straighten this whole mess out." She had read it again, then squealed aloud, picked up the note and noisily kissed it.

"What a guy!" she'd crowed, swelling with joyful optimism. "He'll do it. I know he will!"

She'd come home from Mexico spilling over with hope. Was her cup actually about to overflow? Was she to have everything she wanted? Zach, her painting, even a career?

Then one day passed, and two . . . and now five. Despite the note, she was worried. Where had he gone? Why didn't he contact her?

Suddenly, the frigid water swooshed up aggressively, and her feet disappeared up to the ankles. Yikes, she thought, must be subzero. An ache rocketed up the backs of her legs, and her muscles cramped in protest. She hobbled back to the beach house, hoping Mother Nature wasn't dispensing omens.

* * *

"Eleven days, fourteen hours and forty-two minutes," Trish lamented aloud, sinking down on the window seat. "That's well over 'a few days' by anybody's calendar." Again she scanned the beach obsessively, but by now she couldn't rid herself of the gnawing feeling that he wasn't coming back. The last several days had taught her a lesson in pessimism.

On day six she'd restlessly roamed the cottage. Days seven and eight, she'd propped the telephone on the porch railing and walked the beach—always within hearing distance. At any high-pitched noise—sirens, seagulls' cries, children's whistles—she'd dashed back to check the stubborn instrument. On day nine, she'd called the telephone company. "My phone's out of order," she'd insisted. "It won't ring." When the service department had cheerfully claimed the line was fine, she'd demanded a repairman. Instead, a supervisor's voice had materialized, soothing her as if she were some kind of looney. By the tenth day, she was actually hallucinating. She'd thought she saw him walking up the beach toward her and had run madly toward the approaching figure. It turned out to be a short, rotund man in his fifties, nearly as round as he was tall. When she'd run at him screaming "Zach!" he'd gasped audibly and hurried away.

Now, standing at her living-room window, fingers thrumming against the pane, she vowed, "No longer." It had taken every ounce of her willpower and too much of her sanity to wait this long, but *no longer!* One day, one hour, one second more and she'd be chewing the wallpaper! She had to do something, she *would* do something, but what?

Find him, came the obvious answer. Find *Zach.* She didn't have his phone number, and a quick look through the phone book indicated he wasn't listed, but she knew where he lived.

* * *

The door to his apartment was locked. Trish knocked and called his name, first softly, then louder, and finally so insistently that a neighbor stuck his head out and glared at her. When no one answered, she doggedly descended the creaking steps to the ground floor and found the manager's apartment.

A heavyset, balding man opened the door and surveyed her cautiously. A cigarette hung from his lower lip, and a beer can snuggled in his paunchy fist.

"I'm looking for Zachary Tanner," she asserted nervously. "He lives in 2E, but the door's locked, and he doesn't answer. I'm a friend—"

"He's gone," the man grunted. "Moved out."

A shock wave jarred her. She froze, stunned. After a moment words came out, wooden and hollow. "Where did he go? When?"

"Week or so ago," the man slurred vaguely. "I dunno where he went. He never came down to claim his security deposit. Left his key with the neighbor. Said he was leaving town."

"May I see the apartment?" she whispered hoarsely, too numb to accept the full impact of what she'd just heard.

"Why?" He took a swig of beer.

"I . . . I may want to rent it."

As she went through the apartment, her sense of dread and alienation grew with each empty room. *He was gone.*

The manager paused at the doorway. "Well, lady? Gonna rent or not?"

She couldn't even shake her head. Without saying a word, she brushed rigidly past him and out of the apartment.

"Hey?" he called. "Where you going?"

She didn't stop until she reached the bus stop up the street from the apartment building. A bus lumbered up, its door hissing and clanking open. Not even bothering to check its destination, she hurried aboard.

* * *

"He hasn't left me," she stated quietly. Seated at her kitchen table, she spoke with numb conviction to the empty cottage. "I don't care what it looks like, Zach hasn't run out on me. There's some other explanation for this."

The stillness inside her was almost frightening. After all the tension, shouldn't she be unraveling? But no, she felt deathly calm, almost too rational. When she found him, he'd explain. *When she found him.*

She stared at the hands that were folded tightly in front of her, at the telephone that wouldn't ring a few inches away, at the directory still lying open from yesterday's search for his number.

She resolved to continue to think this through until she had some answers. Never mind that she'd already exhausted the few feasible alternatives for locating him.

After several more moments of futile concentration, a vague memory roused her. The Plymouth . . . where did he get the cab? Independent cabbies either owned or leased their cabs—usually the latter. Zach apparently only used his as a cover for his detective work, so it was probably leased. A rush of anticipation roused her. But no—wait—she'd heard him talking to a dispatcher. Oh, damn, what was the name on the side of the Plymouth? Uni—? United? Something like that. She reached for the directory and leafed through it until she found a listing for taxis. *United Cab Company.* There it was! In downtown L.A.

Fingers trembling, she snatched up the phone and pressed out the numbers. A fragile optimism buoyed her. Moving out of town didn't have to mean he'd gone far away, did it? Maybe he'd simply relocated close by? An adjoining city? Surely the cab company would have records. The dispatchers would know how to reach him.

She crossed her fingers as the phone rang twice, and then a singsong voice came onto the line. "I'm sorry, the number you have called is no longer in service. Please hang up and dial again or . . ."

She dropped the phone. It hit the table with a noisy *thunk,* but the voice droned on. "I'm sorry, the number you have called . . ." With a choked gasp, Trish pushed it away. "Please hang up and dial again . . ."

"Stop it!" she demanded. Pushing the chair back with a screech, she ran from the room.

Hovering out on the porch like a bird poised for flight, she let the gusty winds whip and chill her clear through to her heart. Face it, Trish, you must face it. *He's gone.*

But the wave of grief she'd expected simply didn't come. Instead, a violent shivering overtook her. Her fingers, her limbs turned to ice, and still she stood there in the keening wind.

After several moments, questions began to rush around in her head. Was it true? Was this happening? Had he actually moved away? *Left town?* Without telling her, without a word? After letting her become entangled in this mess and then promising he'd fix everything? Was the man a liar? A shameless phony? Had she been taken in by a pretty face? A con artist?

A saving warmth began to kindle within her. It built to a surge of pure indignation.

"Zachary Tanner," she muttered through clenched teeth. "How could you?"

The grim truth rushed at her as she stood there, eyes narrowing, arms folding tightly. He not only could, he *had,* the bastard!

A sharp inhalation underscored her pent-up emotions. Had he even tried to repair the damage? Or had he simply collected his fee and skipped town? She'd been taken in all right, and royally.

Oh, damn him, *damn him!* Clenching her fists, she exhaled heavily. If she were a dragon, she'd be breathing fire. Boy, but she itched to get her hands on that no-good—!

With two anger-stiffened steps, she crossed the porch and kicked a rattan chair so hard it toppled over. Pain shot through her foot. Oh Lord, it hurt, it hurt! She dropped to the floor and pulled her leather moccasins off. Clutching her stinging toes, she curled up into a ball and rocked back and forth on the hard wooden planks. An angry purple bruise formed underneath the nail of her small toe and crept down, seeping lower under the skin.

"Oh, no, I broke it," she whispered, voice catching. "I broke my little toe—" Her eyes filled with tears. She rocked fiercely, holding her breath. Get up, Trish, she ordered, get up, *get up*. It's just a toe. Why are you blubbering? Don't be so silly, she chided herself, wiping desperately at the tears and swallowing back the sadness that swelled up into her throat. So it stings a little, so what?

Her temples constricted. A dreadful ache seized her chest as she exhaled. *Why did he leave me?* After everything we shared. How could he leave? Oh, Zach, why, dammit, *why?*

Tears trickled down her face and clung to her chin. Struggling to control the welling pain, she angrily brushed them away, pushed herself to her feet and limped to the chair. Righting it, she sat down heavily, elbows on her knees, cradling her head. A poignant sense of loss sharpened with bitter sweetness rocked her. She couldn't believe he'd conned her. Not her Zach. Not the man who'd listened and held her so gently, promised he loved her . . . *crossed his heart* . . .

A heartbreaking sigh trembled on her lips, and her jaw constricted. He hadn't meant to use her, to hurt her. That couldn't be. Oh, no, please, that couldn't be.

"Don't do this, Zach," she whispered hoarsely, as though he could hear her wherever he was. "Don't do this, don't abandon—" The words were lost as an anguished whimper lodged in her throat and then broke free like the sound of a small wounded animal. Unable to stop the torrent, she pressed her hands over the ache in her heart and surrendered to shuddering sobs.

She didn't know how much time had gone by—minutes, hours—when she looked up and saw, through a blur of tears, a lone figure approaching down the beach. Probably the little round man she had frightened half to death the week before. He would really think her a basket case if he came upon her crying her eyes out like this.

She stood up to drag herself inside, but something drew her gaze back to him—a glimmer of gold, the hint of a halo? You've really lost it, girl, she scolded herself bitterly. How many times are you going to repeat the same mistake? Go ahead, go rushing out there in search of your fallen angel. Put your foolish heart on the line again.

Trish dashed the tears from her eyes and peered through the fog and gloom. The man had caught sight of her on the porch and was breaking into a run.

"Zach?" She bounded off the porch onto the beach, paying no heed to the voice of caution or her injured toe. A burst of pain jolted up her leg as her foot hit the sand, but she kept on, her gait a strange hopping hobble.

He caught her in a fierce embrace before she had stumbled twenty feet. A harsh exhalation bathed her face as his hand framed the side of her head, the thumb roughly caressing her cheekbone while fingers splayed and gripped firmly in the wild disarray of her hair. "Are you trying to kill yourself, Mac? Why are you limping?"

"Oh, Zach," she cried, tears welling. "Damn you, damn—" But the last words were smothered as he took her lips so swiftly, so fiercely that all the air in her lungs, in the universe seemed to be sucked into a vacuum of dazzling light. His kiss burned deeply, deeply, warming her heart, touching her soul. Sparks of light exploded behind her closed eyes as she all but lost consciousness.

Wrapping her arms around him, she entangled her fingers in the soft blond curls at the base of his neck. Nothing, no one had ever felt this good to her deprived sensibilities. She soaked up his passion like a desert takes the rain.

"Let me touch you, Mac," he said huskily. "It's been so long." As his hand left her waist to take possession of her breast, his low resonant sounds thrilled her.

"Yes . . . so long," she echoed, her body humming beneath his fingertips.

He lifted her chin, his eyes blue-white and crackling with desire. "Come on," he said, taking her hand and pulling her toward the cottage.

Off balance, she came down on her wounded toe. "Ouch," she said, hobbling. The sharp twinge she felt brought her back from euphoria. The magic of their reunion slipped away as reality edged in. "Wait a minute," she said, holding him off as he tried to pick her up. "Wait a minute." This man left me in the lurch, she reminded herself indignantly. He packed up and moved out of town without a word, and now he's appeared out of nowhere intending to take up as though nothing has happened?

"Where have you been?" she blurted, her voice rustling with emotion. "I've been through hell waiting for you . . . wondering. When you didn't come back, didn't even call, I assumed . . ." She stared up at his burnished face, a face she adored and didn't want to. Her gaze fixed on the pale scar, and she turned away.

He seized her shoulders and brought her back. "You thought I'd run out on you?"

Her silly emotions chose that very moment to overwhelm her restraint. Chin trembling, she said, "What else was I supposed to think?" Her eyes filled and puddled. "It's been twelve days, Zach."

Heaving a sigh, he pulled her into his arms. "I'm sorry, baby. Waiting must have been rough on you." His fingers pressed her lips shut while he explained. "I didn't want to scare you, Mac, but I had to stake out

Anton's place to make damn sure they didn't sneak past me again." His voice grated softly. "Things got a a little more complicated than I expected, but I knew if I told you what was going on you'd worry that I was in danger, maybe even do something crazy like show up at the stakeout. I couldn't take that risk." He kissed her forehead gently. "I'd put you through too much already."

Even as she absorbed his tender apologetic caresses, one of his remarks puzzled her. "You wanted to be sure *they* didn't sneak past you?" she questioned hoarsely. "Who's they? Don't you mean *him*? Anton?"

"No, I mean they. The people I went after were Anton's European buddies, Jacques and Avril."

Trish pulled away. She didn't understand. "Jacques and Avril? What do they have to do with this?"

"Plenty," he asserted. "If not for them, I'd have had the evidence I needed long before I met you. Jacques and Avril are phonies. They're a pair of streetwise Hollywood types I hired to infiltrate Anton's studio and get me the evidence I needed."

"No kidding?" she said, slightly amazed. This did sound like *The Rockford Files*. "So what happened?"

"They decided Anton had more to offer than I did. They took a liking to his lavish life-style and his wild cruises, and decided not to bite the hand that fed them so well." Anger sharpened his features, but his expression softened as he looked down at Trish. "You're shivering," he noted gently. "Come on inside and I'll explain everything."

He led her up the porch and into the living room where it was bright and warm, and pulled her down on the sofa beside him.

"Jacques and Avril," she prompted, urging him to finish his story.

"It took some strong-arming," he admitted, "but once I convinced Nick and Lisa to cooperate, they got me evidence hot enough to send Anton straight to hell."

"Wow," she whispered. "What? What was it?"

"Never mind," he said firmly. "You're too young."

"And your client?" she asked.

"Lydia will get her divorce, all right, and you won't be implicated in the proceedings in any way. I'm sorry you had to be involved in all this, Mac, but I couldn't let Lydia down."

"Lydia? You're on a first-name basis with your client?"

"Have been for the better part of twenty-six years. She's my aunt."

Trish's mouth fell open in surprise. "Your aunt?"

He nodded. "My mother's older sister. She raised me."

Slowly assimilating the information, she questioned, "But . . . your parents?"

"A car accident," he said quietly. "You and I have something in common, Mac. I escaped, too, but with more than a scratch. . . ." His face clouded briefly as he indicated the scars that marred his jaw.

She wanted to touch him, but he looked so remote and distant at that moment, she restrained herself. "Zach, I'm so sorry," she said softly.

"No," he insisted, "it's okay." Through fragments of sadness she saw a smile of considerable strength emerge. "Besides, life with Lydia was like a continual rerun of *Auntie Mame*," he explained. "I had a childhood any kid would envy."

She was inexplicably, almost absurdly glad to know he'd been happy as a child.

"Lydia called me six months ago, desperate for help," he continued. "I'd never understood why she married Anton, so I wasn't surprised when she told me she wanted a divorce."

As he went on, detailing the recent events, Trish began to realize how high the stakes had been for Zach. He'd salvaged his aunt's life as well as her fortune. No small feat, she acknowledged, especially since in doing so, he'd saved Trish McCallister from scandal.

But something lurking beneath Trish's gratefulness

made her question his motives, and even as she tried to stop herself, doubts took hold. Why had he gone to such trouble to find new evidence? Because he loved her, of course, came the defiant answer. But her confidence waned as another possibility occurred to her. Perhaps he'd only wanted to absolve himself of blame? A past like hers elicited sympathy from men— not love. Had he acted out of guilt? Or worse yet, *pity*? Stop it, Trish, you're inventing problems, she warned.

But even as she tried to still the doubts a jarring flashback rushed at her. "I went to your apartment, Zach," she said, her heart thudding heavily. "But you'd moved. Then I called the cab company and—"

"What?" he cut in, forehead wrinkling. He took hold of her shoulders. "Mac, what's wrong?"

"You moved," she accused as though he'd committed first-degree murder. "Your landlord said you'd left town. Why didn't you tell me, Zach?" People in love tell each other things like that, she added silently.

Still baffled, he brushed back his hair. "There wasn't time to tell anybody *anything*, Mac. When I left you in Mexico I went straight to my apartment to get set up for the stakeout. I figured Anton would sic his bodyguards on me, so I packed up and 'left town' to throw them off. As for the cab company, there never was one. I own the cab. It's strictly a cover—"

"But—I heard you talking to a dispatcher," she insisted. Startled, she watched him shrug and fight back a grin.

"That dispatcher is a cassette recording."

"What?"

"Maybe I should explain about the Plymouth?" he offered.

"Please." She didn't like the look on his face one bit.

"The cab was my cover to stake out the Brentmoor," he explained, his eyes twinkling dangerously. "The problem was how to keep fares out of the backseat. I loosened the door handles, and then, just in case, I loaded the backseat with boxes." He shrugged. "Not

179

James Bond, but the best I could do on short notice and a limited budget." His smile became a sly wink. "I wired the dashboard speaker in case a tough customer like yourself muscled in and blew my cover. Not bad, huh?"

"Not James Bond," she agreed uncharitably, bothered by his self-congratulatory tone. How could he be so cavalier? Was all this fun and games to him? Typical dime-store detective stuff? An exciting case, a terrific-looking broad? Had she fallen for a man incapable of commitment to anything more than the thrill of adventure and his immediate hormone count?

She twisted out of his hold and walked to the window seat, folding her arms deliberately. Not once since he'd swept her off her feet down there on the beach had he said or even hinted at the words her heart longed to hear.

"Hey—" He was right behind her, his hand caressing her arm. "What is it? Oh, damn, I know," he laughed, wrapping his arms around her and rocking her gently. "What an idiot I am, it's your career, isn't it? That should have been the first thing out of my mouth." His chin nuzzled in her hair. "Believe me, there's nothing to worry about. With your reputation intact, and the favorable publicity from your first showing, you'll have no trouble finding a new gallery to back you."

"But I have an agreement with Anton," she countered.

"Not anymore," he laughed softly. "I 'persuaded' him to let you out of your contract." His knuckles brushed along her jawline. "He didn't require too much convincing. It seems he's always had a soft spot in his heart for you."

The flash of relief concerning her artistic future faded quickly. Wriggling out of his arms, she moved away.

Zach sounded sincerely puzzled. "Hey, what's wrong? Wasn't that what you wanted to hear?"

Ohh, how could such a damnably clever man be so obtuse? Whirling around, she swallowed her pride and blurted, "What I wanted to hear was, *'I love you,*

Mac.'" Her heart beat wildly, but having said it, she recklessly added, " 'Desperately, deliriously, more than anything else in this world.'" Her jaw tightened and a huge tear rolled down her cheek. Oh hell, why did she always cry when she was angry? So damn *undignified.*

He froze in momentary astonishment, then threw his head back and laughed, a delighted male roar of laughter.

All she could do was stand there as his hand framed her face, lifting it with exquisite tenderness. "Let me rectify that oversight right now," he said huskily and looked full into her brimming eyes. "I love you, Mac. Desperately, deliriously, more than anything else in this world."

His fingers urged her chin toward him, and his lips brushed over hers so vibrantly she yearned for more. With a shaky sigh, she flung her arms around his neck just as he caught them, holding her back for an instant as he added in a low, throaty whisper, "Cross my heart."

EPILOGUE

Where is she? Zach wondered slumberously as he rolled over onto his back. The beach blanket lumped underneath him as he stretched and sat up, blinking away sand and the pale rays of winter's sunshine. The portable easel's half-finished canvas told him Mac had been working while he slept. Maybe she'd gone back in for something to eat?

He stood up, scanned the beach, and when he saw no sign of her, started for the cottage. She's probably hiding in a closet, he thought, smothering a chuckle. She'd been evading him ever since he brought up the subject of their future at lunch yesterday. It hadn't exactly been balm to his ego the way she choked on her tuna sandwich when he mentioned marriage. Well, he was ready for her today. His powers of persuasion would melt her resistance. And if not . . . there was always Plan B.

Finding the cottage empty, he showered, dressed and fixed himself lunch. He was on his second ham on rye when she burst through the back door, arms full of groceries.

"Hi," she said cheerily. "Supplies."

She looked fresh and clean, like an April morning, in her crisp cotton skirt and blouse. And damn sexy. His stomach tightened pleasurably. He watched as she put the groceries away, chatting unself-consciously about her misadventures at the grocery store. There was an enchantment about her, an irresistible something that never failed to excite him. All that energy and enthusiasm gave her a childlike quality that contrasted with and complemented her strength. He shifted in the chair as the tightening in his stomach worked its way lower. Oh, yes, she *was* irresistible.

"Mac, we have to talk. It's time we—"

She stopped him with a frown. "I thought we agreed to postpone any serious talks for a while. To give ourselves a breather?"

They had, but that had been three weeks ago. She'd used the same argument on him yesterday. "A breather, sure, but I'm beginning to hyperventilate."

She handed him a grocery bag. "Breathe into this."

He took the bag and dropped it over his head. "The unknown cabbie," he mumbled, then pulled it off and grabbed her hand. "Come on, Mac," he said, his smile fading. "No more kidding around. It's time we made some plans."

"Okay," she said hesitantly, "but I get to go first. There are some questions I want answered."

"I'm easy." He grinned. "Go ahead."

"Not here," she said, heading for the living room. "An interrogation requires the right environment, and" —she nudged him away as he tried to sit next to her on the window seat—"space. I need room to think."

He took the chair nearest her.

She sobered and began the grilling. "I want to know why you didn't tell me about your past, your aunt, your real motives concerning Anton? Why didn't you trust me enough to tell me what was really going on? You didn't even tell me how you planned to straighten things out. You just disappeared. I know you're a detective and that you believed you were protecting me—maybe that justifies some of your secretiveness, but people in love aren't supposed to make unilateral decisions, Zach. They're supposed to trust and talk and plan—together." Her eyes were soft and sad. "I wish you had trusted me enough to tell me."

"Oh, Mac, you're right," he sighed. "But you've got it backwards, baby." Joining her on the window seat, he sat far enough away to give her the thinking space he could see she still needed, but close enough to take a skein of her long sable hair and let its silky length run through his fingers as he continued.

"I saw the fear and distrust in your eyes the very first night we were together," he said quietly. "Forgive me, Mac, I don't want to hurt you by saying this, but you were waiting, just waiting for me to screw up and prove to you that all men are alike."

She drew away. "What do you mean?"

It wasn't easy, especially with her looking at him that way, but he had to say it. "The pain you've gone through in your life may have taught you a lot about yourself, but it hasn't altered your fundamental perception about men. You still believe men can't be trusted." He hesitated. "Correction—you believe any man who says he loves you can't be trusted. And that includes me."

He nodded a gentle yes when she tried to protest. "Yes, Mac," he insisted. "Maybe not consciously, maybe not even so much now, but on some level, Mac, you still believe it. And dammit, I've been trying to prove your hypothesis wrong." He looked away. "I didn't tell you I was a detective because I was afraid of losing you. I knew that was wrong, so I tried to repair the damage on my own. I knew telling you would only worry or frighten you, and I thought I could fix it without causing you any more pain." He smiled softly and took her hand. "I didn't want to be like the other men in your life, Mac. But maybe I was wrong. Maybe I should have told you everything. Did I hurt you more this way?"

"To tell you the truth," she admitted huskily, tears filling her brown eyes, "I'm so confused I don't care why you did any of it anymore." A moment later, her lips met in a damp smile. "Oh, damn you, Tanner," she said softly. "Why do you always have to be right?"

He scratched his chin thoughtfully. "What day is this, Sunday?"

"Of course not," she said, baffled. "It's Wednesday."

"See." He shrugged. "I was wrong."

"You *are* bad," she muttered, shaking her head.

His heart filled with tenderness as he grinned at her and tried unsuccessfully to keep the twinkles from his eyes. "Now it's my turn to ask the questions. Ready for a little surprise?"

"Surprise?" She straightened warily. "What sort of—"

"Hold it," he insisted gently, pointing to his chest with his thumb. "It's my turn to ask the questions, remember? How do you feel about being *nouveau riche?*"

The glint in her eye told him she had no idea what he was talking about, but she'd play along. "Oh, I suppose newfound wealth has its vulgar compensations. Hopelessly tacky, of course—"

He raised a hand. "Couldn't agree with you more. I'll just tell Lydia to keep her vulgar, tacky money."

Looking utterly shocked, she echoed, "Lydia? What tacky money?"

"The very generous cash gift she insists we accept for saving her fortune."

"Gift? We? Me, too?" Trish broke in. "But I had nothing to do with it. Not directly anyway."

"Ah yes," he sighed, "well, there is one string attached. Lydia lives to meddle. The money's a wedding gift. A little prenuptial bribery, I'm afraid. Lydia's dying to see her favorite and *only* nephew married to the girl he loves."

"A string attached?" Trish gasped. "Sounds more like an industrial cable to me. And whose idea was this wedding business? You only brought up the subject of marriage yesterday. We haven't even discussed it yet."

"That can be remedied."

"No please," she implored. Standing up, she took a step backwards, then another and another until a chair stopped her. "Zach," she blurted, "I have a confession to make."

"Oh no," he groaned. "You're about to tell me you're a nun working for the C.I.A., and your next assignment's in Sri Lanka?"

"I'm about to tell you"—a large gulp interrupted her revelation—"that I'm not twenty-eight years old, not even close."

His eyes crinkled. "If you're under eighteen," he warned, "I'll have to throw you back."

"I'm thirty-four," she disclosed dramatically. "I'll be thirty-five in a month. I'm nearly nine years older than you are!"

The woman totally confused him. She was acting like it actually mattered. "I like a woman in her prime," he quipped, "soft and mellow like ripened Brie."

"Zach, please . . . be serious. I'm talking about *nine* years."

"Nine years, nineteen years." He shrugged. "Don't you know you're the wackiest, most wonderful woman I've ever met? I'd have to be crazy to let you get away."

She pushed back, moving the chair with her. For such a fragile woman, she had remarkable strength. "You're serious?" she breathed.

At his nod she stopped backing up.

"But Zach," she persisted, "marriage is a big commitment. There are so many things to talk about, so many decisions to be made. And I am, after all, a modern woman. I'd want a fifty-fifty relationship."

"You got it."

"I've got it?" she echoed weakly. He saw a swallow move her throat. "Come on . . . ," she parried, flushing, "let's not rush this. There are weighty decisions to be made here. Like . . . where would we live? All these things have to be negotiated." She shrugged nervously. "I'd sort of like to stay here, actually."

"We'll stay here."

Her brows knitted. "Well, then . . . then . . . babies." She smiled triumphantly as though she had him there. "Little teeny babies—you're probably not ready for fatherhood, right? Am I right?"

"I'm ready any time you are," he murmured.

Her reaction was several beats late. "Oh?" She said finally. And then her self-possession crumbled. "Oh, Zach, I do love you, I love you so much it frightens me, but . . . well, I've been through this before, and I'm a little gun-shy."

The woman needed persuading. Time for Plan B.

A secret smile tilted the corner of his mouth as he stood up, lifted his loose-fitting V-necked sweater slightly and pulled a black handgun from the waistband of his jeans. "Never say words like 'gun-shy' to a man who's armed, Mac."

The shock rocked her back, but only for an instant. She took in a deep breath and straightened, squinting suspiciously at the gun. "Where'd you get that?" she questioned. When her eyes met his, they glistened with curious lights. "Tanner, this isn't my idea of negotiating."

"Some things aren't negotiable," he warned, watching a flush creep up her throat and rush warm and pink across her face. His heartbeat accelerated as he said, "Doff the clothes, Mac."

"Wait a minute," she questioned hoarsely. "Is that thing real?"

The gun made an ominous sound as he cocked it.

Her eyes widened. Kicking off her shoes, she began to unbutton her blouse. She looked up once, shy, yet stunningly expectant. Her eyes dazzled him.

The cords in his forearm strained as he worked to keep the gun steady. When he spoke, an odd break roughened his voice. "Want to get married, Mac?"

Her fingers froze on the last button of her blouse. "Is it negotiable?" she asked, her voice low, tremulous.

"'Fraid not." He shook his head, his heart beating hard.

A flurry of seconds rushed past before she looked up, met his brilliant silver eyes and nodded her acceptance.

WIN

a fabulous $50,000 diamond jewelry collection

ENTER

by filling out the coupon below and mailing it by September 30, 1985

Send entries to:

U.S.
Silhouette Diamond Sweepstakes
P.O. Box 779
Madison Square Station
New York, NY 10159

Canada
Silhouette Diamond Sweepstakes
Suite 191
238 Davenport Road
Toronto, Ontario M5R 1J6

SILHOUETTE DIAMOND SWEEPSTAKES
ENTRY FORM

☐ Mrs.   ☐ Miss   ☐ Ms   ☐ Mr.

NAME   (please print)

ADDRESS   APT. #

CITY

STATE/(PROV.)

ZIP/(POSTAL CODE)

RTD-A-1

RULES FOR SILHOUETTE DIAMOND SWEEPSTAKES

OFFICIAL RULES—NO PURCHASE NECESSARY

1. Silhouette Diamond Sweepstakes is open to Canadian (except Quebec) and United States residents 18 years or older at the time of entry. Employees and immediate families of the publishers of Silhouette, their affiliates, retailers, distributors, printers, agencies and RONALD SMILEY INC. are excluded.

2. To enter, print your name and address on the official entry form or on a 3" x 5" slip of paper. You may enter as often as you choose, but each envelope must contain only one entry. Mail entries first class in Canada to Silhouette Diamond Sweepstakes, Suite 191, 238 Davenport Road, Toronto, Ontario M5R 1J6. In the United States, mail to Silhouette Diamond Sweepstakes, P.O. Box 779, Madison Square Station, New York, NY 10159. Entries must be postmarked between February 1 and September 30, 1985. Silhouette is not responsible for lost, late or misdirected mail.

3. First Prize of diamond jewelry, consisting of a necklace, ring, bracelet and earrings will be awarded. Approximate retail value is $50,000 U.S./$62,500 Canadian. Second Prize of 100 Silhouette Home Reader Service Subscriptions will be awarded. Approximate retail value of each is $162.00 U.S./$180.00 Canadian. No substitution, duplication, cash redemption or transfer of prizes will be permitted. Odds of winning depend upon the number of valid entries received. One prize to a family or household. Income taxes, other taxes and insurance on First Prize are the sole responsibility of the winners.

4. Winners will be selected under the supervision of RONALD SMILEY INC., an independent judging organization whose decisions are final, by random drawings from valid entries postmarked by September 30, 1985, and received no later than October 7, 1985. Entry in this sweepstakes indicates your awareness of the Official Rules. Winners who are residents of Canada must answer correctly a time-related arithmetical skill-testing question to qualify. First Prize winner will be notified by certified mail and must submit an Affidavit of Compliance within 10 days of notification. Returned Affidavits or prizes that are refused or undeliverable will result in alternative names being randomly drawn. Winners may be asked for use of their name and photo at no additional compensation.

5. For a First Prize winner list, send a stamped self-addressed envelope postmarked by September 30, 1985. In Canada, mail to Silhouette Diamond Contest Winner, Suite 309, 238 Davenport Road, Toronto, Ontario M5R 1J6. In the United States, mail to Silhouette Diamond Contest Winner, P.O. Box 182, Bowling Green Station, New York, NY 10274. This offer will appear in Silhouette publications and at participating retailers. Offer void in Quebec and subject to all Federal, Provincial, State and Municipal laws and regulations and wherever prohibited or restricted by law.

READERS' COMMENTS ON SILHOUETTE DESIRES

"Thank you for Silhouette Desires. They are the best thing that has happened to the bookshelves in a long time."

—V.W.*, Knoxville, TN

"Silhouette Desires—wonderful, fantastic—the best romance around."

—H.T.*, Margate, N.J.

"As a writer as well as a reader of romantic fiction, I found DESIREs most refreshingly realistic—and definitely as magical as the love captured on their pages."

—C.M.*, Silver Lake, N.Y.

"I just wanted to let you know how very much I enjoy your Silhouette Desire books. I read other romances, and I must say your books rate up at the top of the list."

—C.N.*, Anaheim, CA

"Desires are number one. I especially enjoy the endings because they just don't leave you with a kiss or embrace; they finish the story. Thank you for giving me such reading pleasure."

—M.S.*, Sandford, FL

*names available on request